"I'm perfectly capable of carrying my own suitcase."

"Under normal circumstances, I wouldn't doubt it." Jack picked up the overnighter before Lisa could get to it.

She looked affronted. "You think because I bumped my head that renders me incapable?"

"I didn't mean that. But you planted your car in that ditch pretty good, and you could have a mild concussion. You're what, about six or seven months pregnant, we're stranded in a blizzard, the nearest doctor is more than fifty miles away and between us we've got one horse for transportation. If it's all the same to you, I'd appreciate it greatly if you didn't lift anything any heavier than your hand."

Slowly her brows lowered from their affronted arch and a smile curved those soft lips. "I believe that's the sweetest thing anyone's ever said to me."

"Then, darlin'," he said as he carried her luggage toward the bedroom, "you've been hanging out with the wrong people."

Dear Reader,

Fall is upon us, and there's no better way to treat yourself to hours of autumn pleasure than by reading your way through these riveting romances in September's Special Edition books!

The lives and loves of the Bravo family continue with *The M.D. She Had To Marry,* in Christine Rimmer's popular CONVENIENTLY YOURS miniseries. In the page-turner *Father Most Wanted*, beloved writer Marie Ferrarella combines a witness protection program, a single dad with three daughters and an unsuspecting heroine to tell a love story you won't be able to put down. Bestselling author Peggy Webb deals with family matters of a different kind with yet another compelling Native American hero story. In *Gray Wolf's Woman* a loner finds the hearth and home he'd never realized he'd yearned for.

Lucy Gordon's poignant reunion romance, *For His Little Girl*, will sweep you away as an unexpected turn of events promises to reunite a family that was always meant to be. Janis Reams Hudson continues her Western family saga miniseries, WILDERS OF WYATT COUNTY, with *A Child on the Way,* a compelling amnesia story about a pregnant woman who ends up in the arms of another irresistible Wilder man. And Patricia McLinn's Wyoming miniseries, A PLACE CALLED HOME, continues with *At the Heart's Command,* a tale of a military hero who finally marches to the beat of his own heart as he woos his secret love.

We hope this month brings you many treasured moments of promise, hope and happy endings as Special Edition continues to celebrate Silhouette's yearlong 20th Anniversary!

All the best,

Karen Taylor Richman
Senior Editor

Please address questions and book requests to:
Silhouette Reader Service
U.S.: 3010 Walden Ave., P.O. Box 1325, Buffalo, NY 14269
Canadian: P.O. Box 609, Fort Erie, Ont. L2A 5X3

JANIS REAMS HUDSON

HUDSON

A CHILD ON THE WAY

Published by Silhouette Books

America's Publisher of Contemporary Romance

This book is gratefully dedicated to Sharon Sala, for taking my call every afternoon with such calm good humor. What a friend! You can take your nap now.

SILHOUETTE BOOKS

ISBN 0-373-24349-9

A CHILD ON THE WAY

Copyright © 2000 by Janis Reams Hudson

Visit Silhouette at www.eHarlequin.com

Printed in U.S.A.

Books by Janis Reams Hudson

Silhouette Special Edition

Resist Me If You Can #1037
The Mother of His Son #1095
His Daughter's Laughter #1105
Until You #1210
*Their Other Mother #1267
*The Price of Honor #1332
*A Child on the Way #1349

*Wilders of Wyatt County

JANIS REAMS HUDSON

was born in California, grew up in Colorado, lived in Texas for a few years and now calls central Oklahoma home. She is the author of more than twenty-five novels, both contemporary and historical romances. Her books have appeared on the Waldenbooks, B. Dalton and Bookrack bestseller lists and have earned numerous awards, including the National Readers' Choice Award and Reviewers' Choice awards from *Romantic Times Magazine.* She is a three-time finalist for the coveted RITA Award from Romance Writers of America and is a past president of RWA.

IT'S OUR 20ᵗʰ ANNIVERSARY!
We'll be celebrating all year,
Continuing with these fabulous titles,
On sale in September 2000.

Chapter One

Jack Wilder scrunched his neck down inside the turned-up collar of his sheepskin coat and cursed the weather forecasters for predicting nothing more than a light dusting of snow. He cursed the mountains for not trapping the storm on the western slope and keeping it there. He cursed himself for not heading out of the back country earlier this morning when his left ear started itching—a sure sign something was wrong.

The last time his left ear had itched like this he'd been doing seventy on the highway and nearing a curve. He'd slowed down and thanked God for it a minute later when he came upon a wreck blocking both lanes. If his itchy ear hadn't warned him, he'd have plowed right into both cars and killed everyone.

If he'd paid attention this time, he'd be home. The itch had started about the same time as the snow.

It wasn't merely snowing now. Light dusting, be

damned. What they had here was their first full-fledged, gen-u-ine blizzard of the season. The wind cut through thin clothing and bare skin like a hot knife through butter. The good news, Jack thought with grim humor, was that even if the wind did slice him to ribbons, it would be impossible for him to bleed to death—it was too damn cold for blood to flow.

Skeezer tossed his head and snorted. The fool horse actually enjoyed weather like this.

Visibility decreased by the minute. Jack knew he'd be worse than a fool to try to make it all the way home in this weather when he could stop at the vacant section house. Skeezer would be out of the storm in the barn, and Jack could build a fire in the living-room fireplace, never mind the lack of furniture or electricity.

Jack urged Skeezer over the crest of the final hill and down the other side, where the wind wasn't quite as sharp. The land spread out before him covered in a smooth blanket of white. Acre after acre, mile after mile, even if he couldn't see much of it for the blowing snow. He knew it was there. Flying Ace land. Wilder land. Home.

A thick stand of cottonwoods and willows bordered the creek at the base of the hill. Skeezer waded into the creek, not minding the freezing water, and out the other side. When they broke through the trees, Jack knew the home that normally housed the foreman for the southwest section of the ranch was less than a mile ahead.

Away from the shelter of the hill, the wind sliced with renewed vigor. They trudged on, man and horse, heads down. Jack's fingers, toes and face were going numb by the time the section house appeared before them out of the blowing snow. The house was white, so it was hard to see, but it was there.

If the car had been white, Jack might not have noticed it where it rested nose-down in the ditch next to the driveway. He hadn't expected to see a car. There shouldn't have been one on this road at all, let alone in the ditch. If it hadn't been red and only partially covered with snow, he might have missed it. Some traveler had really gotten lost. Jack just hoped no one was hurt.

He drew Skeezer to a halt beside the car and swung down from the saddle. With his forearm he brushed the snow off the driver's-side window and peered in. His stomach dropped.

The driver was a woman, with a face as pale as the snow. She sat slumped over, with her head against the steering wheel, her ashen face turned toward him, her eyes closed.

Jack rapped on the window. "Ma'am? Lady, can you hear me?"

No response.

He opened the door and felt warm air against his face. Warm compared to outside, anyway. She hadn't been here too long or the interior of the car would have been as cold as the air outside.

How badly was she hurt?

Who was she, and what the hell was she doing out here? Nobody got to this place by accident. She would have had to have turned off the highway and driven under the big Flying Ace sign at the ranch entrance, and then right through headquarters and past the main house. After that it was nothing but miles of rangeland.

Puzzled and concerned, he called to her again while

pulling off his gloves. When he got no response, he reached for her shoulder. God, she looked delicate. Felt delicate beneath his hand, even through her heavy coat. "Ma'am? Come on, honey, wake up."

Still no response.

She seemed to be breathing all right, and when he checked her pulse, it felt normal. Not too fast, not too slow; not thready or weak.

But she was so damned pale. So damned still.

He needed to get her out of this cold, yet he was reluctant to move her until he knew how badly she was injured. From the tire tracks still just visible in the snow, she couldn't have been going very fast. She must have hit her brakes and skidded sideways before landing nose-down in the ditch. The snow already piled up in the ditch would have cushioned the impact. The worst she probably had was a bump on her forehead where she'd hit the steering wheel, and a busted radiator.

He stepped back and eased the car door closed, then jogged through the snow to the front porch. He felt along the sill above the door, found the key and opened the door.

Inside Jack stopped abruptly. "What the...?" The place had furniture, and he recognized it—sofa, recliner, end table, lamp, coffee table... Hell, there was even a small boom box. It was his brother Ace's old stuff from when he'd redone his house a few years ago. Jack had helped cart these things and more to the storage shed. What were they doing here?

Jack himself had gone through this house after the last section foreman had moved out. There hadn't been a stick of furniture here then. Shouldn't be now.

Unless Ace had hired a new section foreman without telling him and supplied the man with furniture.

That didn't make any sense. His brother wouldn't do that. As foreman, second in command over all the Flying Ace ranch, hiring a new section foreman was Jack's job. Ace wouldn't have interfered.

Why was the lamp turned on? The electricity was supposed to be off. And the place was warm. Why was the furnace running?

Jack called out, but got no answer.

Well, the answer to his questions was obvious. The woman must have been expected, and she must be important to someone on the Flying Ace. It would have been no small task to haul all this furniture out here from the storage shed up at headquarters.

Stepping back outside, Jack ducked his head into the wind and trudged back to the car, worried that he'd left the woman alone too long. When he got back to her, she was still out. Reaching into the car, he checked her arms and legs for broken bones, then felt her neck carefully.

She moaned once, shifted her head.

The movement of her head reassured him that her neck wasn't broken. That had been his main concern, and even that hadn't seemed likely.

She moaned again, and her face scrunched up in a frown.

Snow White, he thought, taking in her unnaturally pale face. And again the word *delicate* came to mind. And *beautiful.* Her skin looked as soft and smooth as satin. For a minute he was tempted to stroke one creamy cheek to find out. Or kiss those pale lips…

Bad idea. The woman was unconscious. She wasn't

Snow White, and he damn sure wasn't anybody's Prince Charming. Maybe when she came to…

That idea wasn't much better. For now he just hoped he could rouse her and that she wasn't seriously injured. That he wouldn't do her more harm than good by picking her up and carrying her.

"Ma'am? Can you hear me?"

She heard the deep voice as if through a long watery tunnel. Felt the touch of a warm hand on her shoulder. Confused, she tried to swim back toward the quiet darkness in her mind, but the voice kept calling, insisting she listen, demanding she wake up.

She came to with her forehead pressed against the steering wheel of her car. It hurt. Bad. With a moan, she straightened, leaned back and pressed a hand to the ache, relieved to feel unbroken skin. Boy, it really hurt. A knot was already forming.

How odd that the steering wheel kept coming at her, reaching for her.

No, that wasn't right. It wasn't the steering wheel that was moving, it was her. She kept falling forward. She had to brace herself with a hand on the steering wheel to sit upright.

Frowning, she looked out the windshield to see nothing but white. An icy shiver raced down her spine at the realization that her car—was this her car?—was nose-down in a snow-filled ditch.

Then she turned her head and saw him. The man who had called her from the darkness with his voice and touch.

At first glance he looked like a man she might want a good, close look at. His rugged face was all tanned planes and angles, as if chiseled from seasoned oak by a master craftsman. He wore a tan cowboy hat and a sheepskin coat with the collar turned up. His hair was as black as sin, his eyes as blue as heaven.

A hard-edged man who was easy on the eye.

She blinked and frowned at the thought. She wasn't looking for a man, easy on the eye or otherwise. Didn't want one, wouldn't have one.

The simple movement of frowning shot so much pain through her head that she groaned.

"Ma'am? Are you all right?"

"My head hurts." She blinked up at him. "Who are you?"

"Name's Jack Wilder. You've got a good-size goose egg." He held up his hand. "How many fingers do you see?"

She swallowed. "Three."

"Good. Are you hurt anywhere else besides your head?"

Was she? She frowned again. Her mind was fuzzy and she couldn't quite get it cleared. She felt...strange. Not ill, not hurt—except for the pain in her head. But...fuzzy. Out of focus. As if something wasn't quite right, and she couldn't tell just what that something was. "I think I'm all right."

"It's warm in the house." He reached across her and released her seat belt. "Let's get you inside."

"Oh, okay." She picked up her purse from the passenger seat, pulled the keys from the ignition and dropped them inside. The next thing she knew, the man had swept her up in his arms like a knight rescuing the proverbial damsel in distress. She cried out in surprise.

"It's all right," he said easily. "I've got you."

"I can walk." If her protest sounded a little weak, even to her own ears, well, she was entitled to a moment of weakness, wasn't she? She had just apparently knocked herself unconscious on the steering wheel of her car. Didn't that deserve a little rescuing?

"Not in those shoes, in this snow," he answered. He shifted her easily, as if her weight was nothing to him. Judging by the steely muscles she felt through his heavy coat and hers, it must be.

The sensation of being carried in a strong man's arms was an unfamiliar one. She couldn't recall a single instance when a man had carried her.

Imagine that. Her very own knight in shining…Stetson. She took in his square jaw, his sharp profile, and nearly sighed. Never mind the icy wind, the stinging snow, the treacherous footing. She had the feeling she'd never been safer in her life. "Thank you," she murmured. It was just a crying shame she'd sworn off men.

In no time he carried her through the snow, up onto a small covered porch and into the house. He set her down on the couch, and the first thing she noticed was that the room was blessedly warm. She hadn't realized how cold she'd been.

She started unbuttoning her coat.

"You all right?"

"Yes. Thank you." Without any conscious direction, her hands went to her stomach and started drawing soothing circles there with her fingertips.

The man's eyes lowered, followed the motion of her hands, then nearly bugged out of his head. "You're…"

Shock froze her hands in place. With a hard swallow, she followed his gaze and looked down.

"Oh…my…God." She could do no more than stare at the mound that was her abdomen. Images flashed through her mind. A home pregnancy test. A plus sign on the little tab. A smiling man in a white coat—a doctor?—congratulating her.

Okay. Okay. No need to panic. This was right. She was pregnant. She didn't particularly remember it, but it felt right. *Why didn't she remember it?*

The harder she tried to remember, the worse the pain in her head. Her hands trembled against her stomach.

Stress. It couldn't be good for the baby. She had to calm down, take it easy. Any minute everything would fall back into place.

She closed her eyes and took two slow deep breaths. When nothing came, no thoughts, no memories to explain why finding herself pregnant should come as such a shock, her hands began to shake again.

"...pregnant," he finished.

She let out a puff of breath. "Yes."

His voice sharpened. "You sure you're all right? You didn't hurt anything besides your head, did you?"

"No," she said honestly. "Nothing besides my head." And most of what used to be inside it, she thought, dismayed.

"For a minute there," he said, his voice still sharp, "you seemed a little surprised."

She gave him a nervous smile. "Silly, isn't it? I must have really rattled my brain to have forgotten something like this."

"Will you be all right while I go stable my horse?"

"Sure."

"Do you have any luggage I should bring in?"

"Bring in?" She frowned and glanced toward the door.

"In case you haven't realized it yet, until this storm blows over, we're pretty much stuck here."

She swallowed. "Oh."

Jack bit back a curse. Good God, this was all he needed. A pregnant injured woman on his hands, with a blizzard settling in for the duration, and one horse for transportation. "You're sure you didn't hurt anything when you took that nosedive into the ditch?"

"No." She blinked and curved her hands over her abdomen in that protective possessive way he'd seen other pregnant women do. "No. We're fine."

Jack breathed a silent prayer that she was right, that she and the baby were both fine. He was certainly no stranger to birth, but his experience was with four-legged creatures. This woman didn't look far enough along to be ready to give birth. If she had trouble at this stage, that's what it would be—trouble. With no one to help but him. So she better be fine. She just damned sure better be.

"I'll be back as soon as I've taken care of my horse. You just—" he offered a lame gesture toward the couch, the baby, whatever "—take it easy."

Taking it easy sounded like a good idea, she thought as she watched him step back out into the howling wind. She looked out the window and saw him trudge through the snow to his horse.

She would just sit back and contemplate the uniqueness of having been carried through a blizzard by a gorgeous cowboy.

They were going to get a good laugh out of this when she told…when she told…when she told who?

The name was right there on the tip of her tongue, but it wouldn't come.

Ridiculous. How could she forget the name of her...

Her what? Friend?

Yes, she thought, frowning. It made sense that she would want to tell a friend about konking herself out, coming to in a daze and being rescued by a knight in a cowboy hat.

But how could she forget that name? Why, she knew it as well as she knew her own. All she had to do was relax and let it come. She took a deep breath and let it out. "She's...and I'm..."

Oh...my...God. She did not know her own name!

Her heart leaped, landed in her throat and flopped around fast and hard like a hyped-up fish out of water.

"Easy," she said aloud. "Take it easy." Without thought, she reached into her purse for her cell phone. Finding it, she held it up. The little screen read No Service. She stared at the phone a moment. Obviously she was used to using it. She hadn't thought, *Do I have a cell phone?* She'd simply reached for it as if out of long habit.

No Service.

Striving for calm, she dropped it back into her purse. It really didn't matter, since she couldn't remember who to call. And No Service, no kidding, she thought, looking out the window again at the empty land. What communications company would build a cell tower out here where there were no people? As far as the eye could see—which admittedly wasn't far, what with all the snow—was emptiness. Vast, snow-covered emptiness.

Except for the car. The car that was nose-down in

the ditch and obviously not going anywhere. The car she didn't recognize.

Despite the warmth of the room, she shivered.

Dammit, she knew what a cell tower was, knew she had a cell phone. Why didn't she know what her own car looked like? Or something even more basic, such as the name that had been hers from the day she'd been born? Why didn't she know how old she was? Or where she was?

Think. Think.

Her purse. Surely there was something… Ah, a driver's license. Now she was getting somewhere.

Lisa Hampton. Was that her? Was that her photo?

A mirror. She needed… There. She found a compact and flipped it open. The face that stared back at her made her squeak in shock. It was as unfamiliar to her as Jack Wilder's face had been when she'd come to in the car.

But it matched the photo on the driver's license. The hair was the same—long and thick and auburn. The mouth was the same. The shape of the eyes. Still, it was hard to tell if they were the same person. Driver's-license photos were notoriously bad.

Why did she know that and not her own name?

Okay. *Stay calm.* She was Lisa Hampton. She was twenty-seven years old, her eyes were green— Yes, the ones in the mirror were green. A deep emerald.

Denver. According to the license, she lived in Denver.

She dug through her purse again. Surely something there would trigger a memory, fill in this awful terrifying blankness that threatened to swallow her.

Judging by the gold and platinum credit cards, she

obviously had good credit. Or had had, until she got the credit cards. After that, who knew?

She had a library card. Good for her. And a checkbook that showed a balance of just over a thousand dollars.

Now if only she had a memory. Any memory. Any at all.

Sticking out of a side pocket of the purse was an envelope, unsealed, with the return address of Flying Ace Ranch, Route 2, Box 37, Hope Springs, Wyoming. None of that meant anything to her.

Inside the envelope was a note. It shook in her hand as she read it.

Lisa,

Sorry I missed you. The key to the section house is on the sill above the door. I hope you don't get too lonely out there all by yourself. The phone's shut off, but should be turned on by tomorrow. Take care. We'll be home next week. See you soon.

Love,

B

If she was Lisa, it appeared she had come here on purpose. If this was the section house. Whatever that was.

And she knew someone whose initial was B. Knew her—or him—well, by the tone of the note and the way it was signed.

Love. Did B love her, or was it just a friendly closing, written out of habit?

And good grief, what was she going to tell Jack

Wilder when he came back in and started asking questions?

And just who was this Jack Wilder, anyway, and what was he doing here if *she* was supposed to be staying in this house? If this was the right house.

She had to give him credit for being right about one thing, though—it did indeed appear that they were stuck with each other for the duration of this hellacious blizzard.

A sense of vulnerability threatened to swallow her whole. Somewhere in the back of her mind a voice warned her that he was a man, and men lied. Men cheated. Men did whatever they could get away with to get what they wanted. They did their best to make fools of women, to encourage women to make fools of themselves.

Damnation. What a sucky attitude.

With a gentle hand she stroked the mound of her belly. "I sure hope it wasn't your daddy who taught me to think like that."

Daddy.

There was another thing she couldn't seem to re-call—the father of her child. Why wasn't he here with her? Why had she come to this isolated place alone?

A sense of unease crawled across her shoulders. She would have given almost anything to understand its cause. God, how was she supposed to function without her memory? She had nothing to go on but sheer instinct, and that ugly little voice inside her head that told her not to trust even that much.

Her instinct was to trust this Jack Wilder. Hadn't she felt inordinately safe in his arms as he'd carried her to the house?

But the very fact that she was so willing to trust a

man she'd never met alarmed her. Somewhere in her past she must have learned the hard way not to trust men. That seemed like sound, safe advice, considering she was stuck out here in the middle of nowhere, with no phone, with a stranger. And she was pregnant.

Seven months.

There. A memory. She remembered that she was seven months pregnant. If she remembered that, the rest would come.

Surely the rest will come. Soon.

For now, she would just keep this problem to herself. No sense burdening a stranger with an itty-bitty thing like amnesia. She could always trust him later, after her memory returned. If he proved trustworthy.

For now, she would be on guard.

By the time her rescuing knight came back in bearing a suitcase and an overnighter she didn't recognize, she—*Lisa,* she reminded herself forcefully—was on her feet and ready to fake it for all she was worth.

Since she thought she would have noticed the luggage if it had been on the back of the horse, she assumed he'd retrieved it from her car. She crossed the room toward him. "Thank you. Jack, isn't it? I believe I've forgotten my manners." She held out her right hand. "I'm Lisa Hampton."

With a slight nod, he tugged off one glove and shook her hand. "You picked a heck of a day to go sightseeing."

She looked pointedly out the window. "So it seems."

"How are you feeling?"

"I'm fine. Just a little bump on the head. Along with a bruise to my pride for ending up in the ditch."

"Mind telling me what you're doing out here?"

She arched a brow and smiled slightly while trying her best to ignore the way her insides shook. "I was just going to ask you the same question. You picked a heck of a day to go horseback riding."

"Me?" He pulled off his hat and ran his gloveless fingers through his thick black hair. "I live here."

Startled, Lisa blinked. "Here? In this house?"

"No, but on the Flying Ace. I'm part owner. Were you aware you were on private property?"

Lisa's mind started a mad scramble. The Flying Ace. That's what it said on the envelope she'd found in her purse. She brazened it out. "Of course. I came here on purpose."

"You came to a vacant house on the back side of the ranch during a blizzard on purpose?"

"Well, I hadn't counted on the blizzard." Taking a gamble, she crossed to her purse and retrieved the envelope. "Here," she said, handing it to him. "This should explain."

Curious, Jack took the envelope and stared down at the Flying Ace return address. He pulled the piece of paper from inside, and the light dawned. "You're *that* Lisa—Belinda's friend. That explains the furniture and electricity."

"What do you mean?"

"The section foreman who lived here quit a couple of months ago. Last time I saw this place it was bare as a bone. Belinda must have brought this stuff out for you and had the electricity turned on."

She looked around the room as if in dismay. "She went to a lot of trouble for me."

Jack shrugged. "Why wouldn't she? You're her best friend, right?"

She gave a small jerk, as if someone had just

pricked her with a pin. Or maybe the baby kicked, Jack thought.

"You, uh, know a lot about her."

He gave her a wry grin. "We Wilders are funny that way. One brother generally knows who another brother is married to."

The blink the woman gave him reminded Jack of a confused baby owl. For a minute it seemed that her eyes—or more specifically, the mind behind them—went blank. Then she blinked again and her eyes cleared. She gave him a tremulous smile. "Oh. You're *that* Jack."

He paused. There was something wrong with that smile, but for the life of him he couldn't figure out what. With a shrug, he said, "That's me."

She took a deep breath and squared her shoulders as if preparing to meet some dreaded challenge. "It's a pleasure to meet you. But if you'll excuse me—" she reached for the suitcase beside his leg "—it's been an, uh, eventful day. I'll just go find a place where I can freshen up."

"I'll get it." He whisked up the suitcase before she could grasp the handle.

Slowly she straightened. "Thank you, but I'm perfectly capable of carrying my own suitcase."

"Under normal circumstances, I wouldn't doubt it." He picked up the overnighter as well, before she could get to it.

She looked affronted. "You think because I bumped my head, that renders me incapable?"

"I didn't mean that." Why was it, he wondered, that women were such contrary creatures? "But you planted your car in that ditch pretty good, and the car doesn't have an air bag. You could have a mild concussion. You could have injured something else you aren't aware of yet. You're—what?—about six or seven months pregnant, we're stranded in a blizzard, the nearest doctor is more than fifty miles away, and between us we've got one horse for transportation. If it's all the same to you, I'd appreciate it greatly if you didn't lift anything any heavier than your hand.''

Slowly her brows lowered from their affronted arch and a smile curved those soft lips. ''I believe that's the sweetest thing anyone's ever said to me.''

''Then, darlin','' he said as he carried her luggage toward the bedroom, ''you've been hanging out with the wrong people.''

His voice may have been teasing, but Jack couldn't help but wonder what she was doing out here alone. What kind of man would impregnate a woman, then let her go off into the wilds of Wyoming alone? Where was the man, anyway? Why wasn't he here with her, lifting her suitcase, putting ice on her head, rubbing her shoulders. Holding her. Taking care of her. Making sure she was safe and warm.

Not your business, pal.

And that was the plain truth, he told himself as he strode down the short hall. He checked the back bedroom and found it empty of furnishings, but the front bedroom held a dresser, chest, two nightstands and a king-size bed. He used his shoulder to flip the light switch, then placed the luggage on the bed.

''Thank you.''

Jack turned and found Lisa just inside the doorway. ''You're welcome. While you get settled, I'm going to check out back and make sure we've got plenty of firewood in case we lose power.''

''Is that likely to happen?''

"If this storm doesn't let up soon, it's not only likely, it's probable." Well, hell. He hadn't meant to make her nervous, but from that wary look that came into her eyes, that was exactly what he'd managed to do. "But it's nothing to worry about," he assured her. "The oven in the kitchen is gas. Between that and the fireplace, we'll have plenty of heat."

"Well, then." She clasped her hands together over her stomach, pulled them apart, then clasped them again. "I'm sure we'll be fine."

"Yes, ma'am." He had to assume that if Belinda had gone to the trouble to haul in furniture and turn on the power, she'd surely stocked the kitchen with food. "Nothing to worry about."

With a final nod, he left her there.

Lisa held her breath and watched him go. She listened to the hollow thud of his boots on the oak floor of the hall. Heard the change of tone when he reached the kitchen. Heard the back door open, the wind howl. Heard Jack curse.

At the sound of the back door shutting hard, Lisa jerked. Like a bolt shot home, she flew to the bedroom door and closed it, pressing her back against it and squeezing her eyes shut.

Why was this happening to her? Why couldn't she remember?

In desperate fear of forgetting the few things she had just learned, she silently repeated them to herself.

Her name was Lisa Hampton, she was from Denver, and she was seven months pregnant.

She was Brenda—no, Belinda—Wilder's best friend, and Belinda was a generous person.

Belinda's husband had a brother named Jack, who

liked to take charge, seemed genuinely concerned for Lisa's welfare, and had eyes as blue as heaven.

"Oh, great," she muttered. With everything that was going on, she had to get hung up on a man's eyes.

Shaking her head at herself, she steadied her nerves and crossed to the suitcase. Maybe something there would jog her memory.

She got a jog, all right. Not to her memory, but to her heart when she opened the suitcase and found enough cash to choke an elephant. Twenties, fifties, hundreds, all stuffed into a black duffel bag beside her clothes.

A violent trembling seized her. What had she done? Good Lord, what had she done? Why was she carrying so much cash when there was clearly no place around to spend it?

Running, came the thought. *Hiding.*

From what? From whom? From someone she might have stolen it from?

Her heart was pounding so hard and fast that she had to sit on the bed and wait for her pulse to slow before she could think past the shock of finding the money. Gradually her heartbeat slowed, as did her breathing. After all, she thought, what was a little unexplained money when she couldn't remember her own name?

Lisa Hampton. Lisa Hampton.

But why didn't it sound familiar?

From beyond her closed door she heard the kitchen door open and close again, heard the thump and thud of heavy boots on the floor.

On the outside chance that Jack Wilder might come into the bedroom, she quickly started stuffing handfuls of money under the mattress. Even with no memory, she knew that hiding place was worse than a cliché, but short of just tossing it into an empty dresser drawer, she couldn't think of anyplace else to hide it.

And she wanted it hidden. From Jack, from herself. Out of sight, out of mind. Since she didn't know what she was doing with that much cash—roughly seven thousand dollars, she'd counted—she didn't want to think about it. It was just one more giant question mark in the black void of her memory.

With that chore finished, she looked through the rest of her suitcase, hoping against hope that something would trigger a memory. Even a small one would help ease the tightness in her chest.

She wondered what it said about her that she felt relieved that the clothes she found—slacks and matching tops, all of the maternity variety, of course—were made of solid-colored fabrics, cut in simple lines. No frills or froufrous, no ruffles or bows. Good for her. She liked that.

She did wonder about the colors, though, all browns and greys and dark greens. Did she not like red? Yellow? Berry?

Ah, there was the color. Bras and panties in every shade of the rainbow, from startling red to pastel peach—even if the panties, with their wide elastic insets, were large enough to accommodate an expectant moose. She figured they ought to just about fit her. And here, she didn't mind the lace. Rather liked the idea of it being hidden next to her skin, for her own private enjoyment.

There was one pair of maternity jeans, and a long-sleeved, bell-bottomed sweatshirt with bold black letters emblazoned across it proclaiming, "Yes, I'm smuggling a basketball." And tucked into a corner beneath a long terry-cloth bathrobe and blue flannel nightgown, a pair of bright yellow Tweety Bird slippers.

So, Lisa Hampton had a sense of humor. That was a relief. Smiling, she slipped off her loafers and tugged on the slippers.

She rifled through the overnighter, pursing her lips at the cosmetics she knew—without knowing how she knew—were top-of-the-line and expensive. Setting it out on the dresser, she went back to the suitcase and found a large manilla envelope beneath the last of her underwear. Inside were her medical records from her obstetrician in Denver.

Good grief, why would she bring her medical records? Unless she wasn't planning on returning.

And what, she wondered, did the money have to do with this?

She was still asking herself these questions when a knock sounded on the bedroom door.

Startled, she jumped and placed one hand over her heart, the other over her abdomen.

"Lisa?" Jack called.

She crossed to the door and opened it. "Yes?"

He had removed his coat and boots, and stood in his stockinged feet, the open collar of his blue plaid flannel shirt revealing the crew neck of a white T-shirt. The shrug he gave her was charmingly self-conscious.

"I, uh, just wanted to make sure you hadn't gone to sleep. With a head injury..."

She couldn't help but smile in appreciation and

gratitude at his concern. "No, I'm awake. Thank you for checking."

"I checked the kitchen, too. It's pretty well stocked. Are you hungry?"

She started to answer, but her stomach rumbled and beat her to it.

Jack grinned. "I guess that means yes."

It was her turn to be self-conscious. She laughed. "I guess it does." She flipped off the bedroom light and followed her knight to the kitchen.

She came to the conclusion that this man was comfortable with himself. It showed in the easy way he moved and walked, the confident carriage of his head, the straightness of his shoulders. Comfortable, and sure of himself and his place in the world.

Had she ever felt like that? Was Lisa Hampton comfortable with herself and her place in the world? Did she love the father of her child? Did he love her? If so, why did she get this disconcerting tightness at the base of her skull every time she thought about the man—whoever he was?

Because she had no answer to that and the possibilities were limitless, the father of her baby went the way of the money in her suitcase. Out of sight, out of mind. She stuffed him under a mental mattress, determined not to think about him for now. He obviously wasn't here with her, where he belonged. Didn't a father-to-be belong with the mother-to-be?

On the other hand, maybe she had left him. Maybe that was why she was here alone.

Or maybe she had done something outrageous, such as robbed a liquor store in order to run away and meet him so they could flee the law together and raise their child on the run.

God, she had to stop this or go crazy.

"What are you hungry for?" Jack asked her.

Startled, she jerked her hands up to her abdomen. "Oh. Anything, really. Anything at all."

Jack noticed the way she had jumped at the sound of his voice. Noticed, too, that wary look in those emerald-green eyes. He couldn't say he blamed her, a woman in her condition, alone, stranded in the middle of nowhere with a strange man.

He wanted to tell her he wasn't strange, that he was no threat to her. But then, if she believed every man who came along and said, "Trust me," she'd be a fool, and Lisa Hampton didn't seem like a fool to him.

Besides, she was Belinda's best friend, and Belinda wouldn't give the time of day to a fool.

To help ease some of her worry and tension, he kept his voice friendly, relaxed. "How about we stick with something fast and easy this time, like soup?"

"Sounds good. What can I do?"

"You can sit down and put your feet up. Pregnant women and car accidents don't mix well."

"I'm fine," she told him. But she pulled out a chair at the table and sat.

Jack appreciated it, even if she was only humoring him. He wasn't going to be able to quit worrying about her and that baby until he got them into town to the doctor. And that, judging by the way the storm was strengthening outside, was not going to be anytime soon.

"Chicken noodle or tomato?" he asked.

She stared at him blankly for a moment, then blinked. "Either one is fine."

"Okay, then I'll surprise you."

There obviously hadn't been a spare microwave in storage when Belinda furnished this place for Lisa, so Jack had to heat the soup—chicken noodle, he'd decided—the old-fashioned way, in a pan on the stove.

"Nice shoes, by the way," Jack told her while waiting for the soup to heat.

She held out one foot and rotated it. "Thank you. They do make a fashion statement, don't they?"

Jack chuckled at the big cartoon birds adorning her feet. "They make some kind of statement, I'm sure."

While the soup heated, Jack went to the living room and turned on the television in hopes of catching a weather report. All that was on was football. He kept the volume on low.

As soon as the soup was hot, Jack poured it into bowls and carried the bowls to the table. At her first taste, she reared back, looked at her spoon and smiled, as though pleasantly surprised.

"Something wrong?" he asked.

"No. It's delicious."

They didn't speak again. They were both too hungry, too busy eating. The only sound was the music of spoons clicking on porcelain, the occasional creak of a chair from the shifting of weight and the faint murmur from the television.

Over all these mundane sounds was the constant howl of the wind outside the snug little house.

When they finished eating, Lisa let out a sigh. "I was hungrier than I'd realized. Thank you. It was just what I needed. Brenda went to a lot of trouble to stock food for me."

Brenda? Jack forced himself to appear relaxed. He scooted his chair back and turned it sideways so he could stretch out his legs without getting tangled up with the chair legs beneath the table.

"Yeah," he said easily, watching her closely. "That's Brenda for you."

The smile she gave him bordered on nervous and flitted away quickly. "She never changes."

"Nope. Same ol' Brenda. Still tall, still forty pounds overweight. Still got that long blond ponytail clear down her back."

Another nervous smile. "That's her."

"That's bull."

She blinked. "Pardon?"

"In the first place," Jack said, his voice turning cold and hard, "your *best friend's* name is Belinda, not Brenda. In the second, she's short, thin and has short dark hair. Now suppose you tell me who you really are, what you're doing here, and what you've done with the real Lisa Hampton."

Chapter Two

Panic came into her eyes. Panic, and tears. "Wh-what do you mean?"

"Cut the crap, lady." He would not let her tears get to him. "You looked me square in the eye and lied. You ought to be able to look me in the eye and tell me the truth. Who are you?"

"But I *am* Lisa Hampton," she cried, her hands curling into fists, her tears threatening to overflow. "I'm *sure* I am."

Jack paused in the act of leaning forward. "You're *sure* you are? What the hell is that supposed to mean?"

Her eyes widened, as though she hadn't meant to say those last words aloud. "I…"

"Come on, talk to me."

"I'll prove it." She pushed herself from the chair. "Prove what?"

"That I'm Lisa Hampton." Her lower lip trembled even as she sucked back her tears. "Just wait." She dashed out of the kitchen.

Jack started to jump up and follow her, but he reminded himself that she couldn't go far. Not in this weather. He heard her go down the hall and into the bedroom. A moment later, slightly out of breath, she was back in the kitchen.

"Here." She thrust a wallet at him, held open to show him a driver's license. "Lisa Hampton. That's me."

Jack looked at the license. The name was sure enough Lisa Hampton, and the photo was probably her, although with those damn mug shots that ended up on most licenses, he supposed it could be a picture of someone else. But no, he thought again, that was her.

"It's me, isn't it?"

Jack did a double take. "What do you mean, isn't it?"

His question plainly startled her. "Oh. I mean...I just meant, see? It's me. Lisa Hampton."

With suspicion doing a tap dance up and down his spine, Jack studied her with narrowed eyes. Something wasn't quite right here. He'd thought she'd been lying earlier. Right now she didn't look as if she was lying—she looked...uncertain. "Is it?" he asked in response to her statement. "Are you really Lisa Hampton?"

"Why are you doing this?" she cried. "Why don't you believe me?"

"I told you why. You claim to be best friends with a woman whose name you can't remember. You don't know what she looks like. Why is that? If you're Lisa

Hampton, why don't you know your own best friend?''

Lisa squeezed her eyes shut and fought tears of frustration. What was the use? She obviously wasn't fooling him. If only she didn't feel so…lost. Lost to herself. Her voice, when it came, was a whisper of anguish. "I don't remember."

"You don't remember your best friend?" he scoffed.

"I don't remember *anything,*" she cried.

Jack stared at her, dumbfounded. There was no denying the anguish in her eyes, or the fear. But fear of what? Of being caught in a lie?

That didn't make any sense. Why would she lie about a thing like this?

"Nothing?" he asked.

"Nothing." Her voice shook. "Not my name, not what I'm doing here or how I got here. Not even my face," she added with despair, "when I look in the mirror."

"Good God." Women weren't at the top of the list of people Jack trusted, but he couldn't help but believe her. Still, he couldn't stop himself from repeating. "Nothing?"

"*Nothing.*" And then she buried her face in her hands and cried. Great racking sobs that seemed to be torn from her depths.

His heart squeezing, Jack rose swiftly and, with a hand to her shoulder, guided her back to her chair at the table. More than one woman, from his mother on down, had tried to manipulate him with tears, but not even his mother at her worst had ever sounded so…lost. It got to him. He couldn't deny it.

She didn't seem to mind his hand on her shoulder,

so he left it there. He told himself it was for her benefit, that it might help her to know she wasn't alone.

It did help. Through her tears, Lisa was grateful to know that Jack Wilder was kind enough to comfort a hysterical woman. His touch was so warm and strong, so sure and certain, she wanted to fling herself into his arms and hide there until her world righted itself and she could look in the mirror and know who she was.

The urge to turn to him dried her tears as no amount of comforting words could have. Good grief, she hoped she wasn't the type of woman who needed a man to cling to.

"I'm sorry," she managed.

"For what?"

It wasn't his voice that startled her, but that it came from right beside her ear. She hadn't realized he was crouching beside her chair, but when she turned her head, they were eye to eye.

She let out a nervous puff of breath. "For falling apart like that."

He gave a small shrug. "From the sound of it, I'd say it's been building up for quite a while. You needed to get it out."

She sniffed. "I wish I knew."

"And I wish we could get you to a doctor. That bump on your head must have done more damage than we realized."

Lisa pressed her fingers to the knot on her forehead and winced.

Jack took her hand and brought it down to the table. "I'll tell you what I tell my nephews—don't play with it."

Reluctantly, but unable to help herself, she smiled. "Are you telling me I'm being childish?"

"No."

The softness in that deep voice started a melting sensation in her bones. For a long moment all she could do was look into those bright blue eyes. What was the matter with her? Her entire life had been wiped from her mind, and she was being pulled toward this stranger like the proverbial moth to a flame.

She forced herself to blink and look away, breaking whatever spell had held her in its grip. "How old are these nephews of yours?"

He stood and carried their empty bowls to the sink. "Well, let's see. Jason's the oldest, at seven. Then there's Clay, who's five, and Grant is three. Those are Ace and Belinda's boys. Cody, my sister's new stepson, is five."

"Belinda has three sons?"

Jack finished rinsing the bowls and turned to look at her. "They're her stepsons. And her nephews."

Lisa blinked. "How does that work?"

Jack chuckled. "It's confusing, but it works fine. Ace was married to Belinda's sister, Cathy. Cathy died—" Jack cut himself off. He didn't think it would be a good idea to tell a pregnant woman about another woman dying in childbirth. No sense putting a fear like that in her head. "And a couple of years later, Belinda came for the summer to help him take care of the boys. She and Ace ended up married."

"It sounds like you've got a big family."

"Big enough. Two brothers, one sister."

"It must be nice," she said wistfully.

"Does that mean you're an only child?" he asked casually.

She opened her mouth to answer, then closed it with a frown. "I don't know. I... It was there. I knew the answer. Then it was gone. Just...poof. God, this is driving me crazy. Why can't I remember?"

"You will," he told her. "You probably just knocked your marbles loose today out there in that ditch. Don't try to push it. It'll come."

She arched a brow. "You have a lot of experience with amnesia, do you?"

"No, but it's just common sense. I like to think I have enough of that to get me by."

Lisa let out a harsh breath. What good would it do her to pick a fight with him? He was, after all, the only person on the planet she could truthfully say she knew.

Now there was an unsettling thought. Better to get her mind on something else. Anything else. "Your family. Belinda's family. Do I know any of them? I mean, besides Belinda."

Jack heard the wistful tone in her voice, and he had to fight the urge to cross the room and offer whatever comfort he could. What was it about this woman that kept filling him with the desire to wrap his arms around her and hold on?

"No," he said in answer to her question. "I don't think so. I just remember hearing her talk about you now and then."

"Was it good, what she said about me?"

"You're her best friend."

"Does that mean I'm a good person, do you think?"

It struck Jack as appalling that she didn't even know that much about herself. No wonder that fear lurked in her eyes. He offered her a smile. "You must be okay. I don't think bad people wear cartoon characters on their feet."

"Well," she said with an answering smile, brief though it was, that almost, but not quite, chased the fear from her eyes. "There is that."

Jack turned back to the sink and, for something to do, decided to wash the few dishes they'd used.

When Lisa saw what he was doing, she rose and started opening drawers.

"What are you doing?"

"Looking for a dish towel. You're washing, so I'll dry. But really, you cooked, so I should clean up."

"There. We just learned something else about you. You're not lazy. You don't expect people to wait on you."

"I should hope not!" she exclaimed.

"And you have fairly strong opinions about how people should behave," he added with a grin.

"I do?"

"I'd say so, judging by your response just now." He rinsed a bowl and handed it to her.

Frowning in thought, Lisa took the bowl and dried it. When she finished with the second one, she opened a cabinet door, looking for the place they belonged. Instead of dishes, she found groceries. A box of cereal sporting a cartoon tiger.

They're grrr-eat!

Lisa whipped her head around, certain that someone had just shouted the words in her ear.

"What?" Jack asked. "Is something wrong?"

There was no one in the room with her except Jack. Frowning, she looked back at the cereal box. "Tony."

"Who?"

"The tiger on the box. His name is Tony."

Jack pulled the plug on the sink. Water gurgled down the drain. "Yeah, so?"

Lisa gripped the handle on the cabinet door until her knuckles turned white. "So how do I know that, when I don't know my own name? How do I know that if I turn the box next to it around, there'll be three little guys on it named Snap, Crackle and Pop, or that the brand of coffee sitting next to it promises to be good to the last drop? How do I know these things? *Do* I know them, or am I making them up?"

"You're not making them up. You're remembering carefully planned advertising campaigns designed to embed themselves in your unconscious mind. I'd say they worked."

Dismayed, she looked at him. "Ad campaigns?"

"That's right. Slogans. Tag lines. Brand-name identification. Whatever they're called. You've been bombarded with them—everyone has—every time you've turned on the television or radio since the day you were born."

She shook her head and closed the cabinet door. "Of all the things to remember."

Jack shrugged. "You remember how to walk, how to talk, how to use a spoon, dry dishes. The way I see it, the only things you don't remember are personal things, about you. At least, that's the way it happens in the movies."

"The movies? Gee, thanks, Dr. Wilder, for that considered medical opinion. If I were a movie, I could watch myself and fill in all these blanks in my head. I feel more like a videotape that's been bulk-erased."

Watching her closely, Jack picked up the bowls she

had dried and put them in the lower end cabinet. "Bulk-erased?"

She gave a negligent shrug, searched for and found the silverware drawer and put their spoons away. "As opposed to simply recording black over a section of the tape. You put the tape on this machine that's basically a giant magnet, and it erases the whole tape at once. Presto. Bulk-erased."

"I guess you've got one of these bulk-erasers at your office, huh?"

"I…" She stopped and pressed her fingers to the knot on her forehead. Her eyes scrunched shut, her face paled. "I don't know." She dropped her hand and looked at him, her eyes accusing him of something he wasn't sure he understood. "Why did you ask me that when you know I don't remember anything?"

He tossed the dishrag over the divider in the sink. "You were on a roll. You weren't thinking about what you were saying. It was just coming out. I thought maybe more would come if you didn't stop to think about it."

He was right, she realized. She hadn't had to think about it. She knew what videotape was, could see it in half-inch, three-quarter-inch and one-inch formats. In black plastic cassettes and on metal or plastic reels of various colors. She could hear the whir of tape machines, the buzzing hum of the bulk-eraser.

"Why do I know all of that, but I don't know if I even have an office?" Frustration was eating a hole in her chest. "I don't seem to know anything about myself, but I know it's Sunday because there's a stopwatch ticking on the television and I hear Morley

Safer's voice, so *60 Minutes* is on. Which means it's Sunday. Six o'clock, unless there was a ball game that ran long.''

Jack nodded. ''You're right. It's Sunday.''

''I *have* to know more than this. I have to remember. My purse,'' she murmured. ''Maybe there's something else…''

Jack watched, frowning, as she headed back to the bedroom in those ridiculous yellow slippers. He had a hundred questions he'd like to ask her.

If he had that many, he shuddered to think how many she had. He couldn't begin to imagine what it would be like not to know his own name, his family, where he was from, what he did for a living. What kind of man he was.

She returned, muttering to herself, one hand buried halfway up her forearm in her brown leather purse. With a growl like a frustrated kitten, she dumped the contents on the table.

Jack shook his head in wonder. ''Why is it that women feel the need to carry so much junk around with them all the time?''

''Because we never know when we might need it,'' she muttered.

''Does anything look familiar?''

She fingered a tube of lipstick, played with a black plastic comb. ''I know what it all is, but…'' She shook her head. ''None of it means anything to me.''

''What's this?'' Jack picked up a small flat brass case.

''A business-card holder,'' she muttered. Then her face lit up. ''I have business cards.'' She snatched it out of his hand and popped it open. The cards read:

Lisa Hampton
Broadcast Producer
Walter and Thompson, Denver

"What's Walter and Thompson," Jack asked.

"It's an ad agency. A national agency—no, world-wide. They have offices all over the world. I know that, know what W&T is, so why don't I remember anything about it? Like working there?"

When she looked up at him, Jack would have given anything to be able to answer her questions and take away that look of lost vulnerability in her eyes. But all he had to offer was a lame, "It'll come back to you."

"Will it?"

"Sure. Just give it time."

"But what if it doesn't come back?" She thumbed the business card, looked at the contents of her purse without a hint of recognition. "What if I never re-member?"

"Hey," he said softly. Without thinking, he reached out and stroked her cheek. Warm satin. "Don't go borrowing trouble. You've had an acci-dent, probably have a mild concussion, and that's what's causing your memory loss. Considering the other side effects of a concussion, you're not in too bad a shape."

"You mean amnesia is the good news?"

"I don't know that I'd call it good, but at least you're not suffering from nausea or double vision or fainting spells. You're not in a coma. Your pupils look the same size in both eyes, so you probably don't have a blood clot in your brain. Do you want me to go on?"

"I thought you were a cowboy. Why do you know so much about all this?"

"Because of those nephews I told you about. And my brothers. Somebody around here is always getting conked on the head by one means or another. You learn to recognize the symptoms."

She just stood there, looking up at him, bewildered.

Jack had the deepest urge to pull her into his arms and hold her close, tell her not to worry, tell her everything would be all right. Tell her he would take care of her.

He fought it. Fiercely.

That he had to fight it shocked him. He couldn't remember a woman ever pulling at him this way before. Jack liked women as much as the next guy did, but he preferred women who didn't have hearth, home and family written all over their face, and that's just what he read on Lisa Hampton's face. He didn't know what to do with women like that, except steer clear of them. They always seemed to want something from him that he didn't have within himself to give.

Lisa finally looked away. She started gathering her things back into her purse. "If you don't mind, I think I'd like a hot bath."

"Fine." He cleared his throat. "That's fine. When you're finished, I'll take a shower. I think I smell like my horse."

Her smile was brief and tentative. "You smell like a very nice man to me. Thank you, Jack Wilder. I don't know what I'd have done if I had come to and found myself alone."

"Oh, I don't know," he told her, feeling at ease again with her. "I think you would have managed just fine."

"I'm glad I didn't have to find out."

* * *

Lisa had her bath, then settled in the living room. The television programs were all right, but it was the commercials that fascinated her.

When Jack got out of the shower, he dressed in jeans and his last clean shirt, which had been in one of his saddlebags.

Belinda hadn't anticipated that there would be anyone here but Lisa, so he took care to hang his towel on the shower rod to dry. If they were stuck here for more than a couple of days, they would have to do laundry. Which would be a problem since there was no washing machine or clothes dryer. How long would it take a sopping wet towel to dry, particularly if the electricity, thus the central heat, went off?

He didn't hold out much hope for the electricity if this damn storm didn't move out soon. The lines were bound to be coated with ice; it had rained before it started snowing. Enough ice on the power lines, and down they would go.

He had told Lisa what they could expect in that regard. After his shower he'd cleaned the tub and filled it with water, because without electricity, the well would shut off. While she'd been in the tub, he'd gone out to the well house and checked the old hand pump. It still worked, so they would at least be able to haul water to the house. They wouldn't be without.

While he'd been out there, he'd filled two five-gallon buckets and carried them into the kitchen, just in case. The way he figured it, there was no sense waiting until he was thirsty to go looking for water.

Now they were as set as they could be. He'd even checked the batteries in the small boom box Belinda had left for Lisa in the living room, so they would be able to listen to the outside world if they could pick up a signal through all this damn snow.

He stepped into the living room and stopped in the doorway. Lisa was there, on the couch. She still wore those crazy slippers. But instead of the dark gray slacks and matching top, she now wore a fuzzy blue robe that was primly buttoned from her ankles to her chin. Her face was scrubbed clean of any makeup. With her fingertips, she unconsciously drew circles across her abdomen.

What would it be like, Jack wondered, for a man to have a woman like this waiting for him at the end of the day. A soft beautiful woman. A child—his child, their child—on the way. A family. His family. He would stroke her belly, feel the baby move. She would rub his shoulders. They would talk and laugh, hold each other through the night. Face each day, the good ones and the bad, together, side by side.

Jack shook his head. What was the matter with him, thinking like that? He knew better. That dream wasn't for him.

It wasn't that he didn't believe in love. He did believe in it, strongly. So strongly that he had practically taken matters into his own hands to make sure Ace and Belinda looked past the blinders they'd been wearing to realize they were in love.

Yeah, Jack believed in love, all right. Just not for himself. Oh, he'd tried a time or two, but it just didn't seem to be in him to love a woman. He figured he came by that little flaw in his character naturally. Not only had he learned at an early age that his own mother resented his very existence, she hadn't even liked herself. He never learned to receive or give love, and if there was a love gene, the woman who'd given birth to him hadn't possessed it, and therefore had not passed it along to her only son.

But that didn't mean he couldn't dream. And he had a feeling that tonight he was going to dream of auburn hair, green eyes and skin as soft as satin.

He realized he'd been standing in the doorway, watching her, for far too long. But she hadn't seemed to notice; she was engrossed in the television.

A moment later he felt his lips twitch. It wasn't a program that held her so enthralled, it was the commercials. Now she was reciting an automobile ad word for word along with the television.

"Was that one of yours?" he asked when the spot ended.

"Oh." At the sound of his voice, Lisa gave a start. She hadn't intended to stay in the living room so long and let him catch her in her robe. What must he think? She must look like Shamu the Whale, dressed by Omar the Tentmaker. "I'm sorry. I didn't know you were there."

She started to push herself from the couch and go to her room, but instead, told herself to relax. She *did* look like Shamu, and her giant fuzzy bathrobe was big enough to house an entire desert tribe. There was no way he could think she was issuing any kind of invitation just because she happened to be in her gown and robe. And even if he thought she was, he would laugh himself silly at the idea of a seven-months-pregnant woman thinking she could entice a man.

Who wanted to entice a man, anyway? She certainly didn't. Judging by the shape she was in, she'd already done that.

It troubled her greatly that she had no memory of her baby's father. Surely if she loved him, she would feel something, wouldn't she? Some whisper of love, of missing him?

But there was nothing. Not a shred of feeling.

Why? she wondered. How could she forget a man she loved enough to make a child with?

"Is something wrong?" Jack asked from the doorway.

"Oh. No. Sorry. What were you asking? Something about one of mine?"

"The ad. You were reciting it line for line. I wondered if it was one you'd done."

Lisa took in a slow deep breath and told herself to relax. This constant questioning of herself made her tense, and that wasn't good for the baby. "I don't know," she said in answer to Jack's question. "I just knew the words. Silly, isn't it? I didn't know if I liked chicken noodle soup, but I know the entire script of a TV commercial."

Jack shrugged and sauntered into the room. "It's what you do. You probably spend all day every day working on commercials. I'm guessing that's how you met Belinda."

"How?"

"She used to work in advertising."

"Really? Where?"

He shook his head. "I don't know. Somewhere in Denver. When she came here last spring, she had her own business designing Web sites. She brought it with her. Has an office upstairs at the house."

Lisa started to comment, but a new commercial caught her eye. "Oh, look. I know this one. Man's best friend. The dog is going to make a sandwich, but they're out of the right kind of spread.''

Jack wasn't a big TV fan. He was even less of a fan of commercials. But this one was clever and funny.

It was as if the storm, too, had been watching, waiting for the spot to end before kicking in to make things more interesting. The instant the spot was over, the electricity went out. The room, the entire house, was plunged into complete darkness. And silence. Except for the howl of the wind.

Chapter Three

"Jack?"

"Stay put. I'll be right back."

"Where are you going?"

He heard the nervousness in her voice and paused. "I'm going to get the lantern in the kitchen, then I'm going to start a fire. Don't move. It's black as the inside of a hibernating bear in here."

Lisa clamped her jaws shut to keep from asking him not to leave her alone. Did this mean she was afraid of the dark? How...distressing. How wimpy. She didn't like to think of herself as a wimp. An adult who was afraid of the dark. A woman who had to have a man to lean on, to take care of her.

Maybe it wasn't the dark that had her nerves stretched taut. At least not only the dark. There was the wind, the howling wind that sounded as if it had teeth and would rip away the walls any minute. And there was this damned black void in her head, which, on its own, swamped her with a hated feeling of help lessness.

From the kitchen came the glow of a flashlight, then, a few minutes later, the brighter glow of a gas lantern.

Jack carried the lantern to the fireplace, where he knelt and lit the kindling waiting there beneath several logs.

The light was a relief to Lisa. The heat, too, even though the room was plenty warm from the furnace that had been running. At least now she knew it would stay warm.

Crouching on one knee, Jack swiveled to face her. "You okay?"

"Fine. I'm fine. Thank you."

"You already thanked me."

Lisa shook her head. "Not for this."

"One thanks is enough."

"No," she said. "It will never be enough."

"It's plenty." He rose and dusted bits of bark from his hands. "You said thanks, I'll say you're welcome, and we'll call it done. All right?"

"All right. For now. But I reserve the right to thank you again, the next time you do some-thing...thanksworthy."

"Thanksworthy?" Jack's lips quirked up at the corners. "Is that a real word?"

Lisa smiled. "I have no idea, but if it's not, it should be, don't you think?"

As the flames devoured the kindling and bit into the logs, Jack shook his head at her question and turned the knob on the lantern until the hiss and glow ebbed sharply, then cut off.

"No telling how long the power will be off, and what fuel is in there is all there is. We'll save it for when we really need it."

The fire lent an intimate glow to the room, and the smell of wood smoke teased the air.

In direct contrast to the soft pleasant atmosphere, the sound of the blizzard pulled on Lisa's nerves. "I wonder how deep the snow is by now."

"When I went out to the well house, it was six to eight inches, where it wasn't drifted up a foot or more. We'll see a foot or two before this blows out. Does it worry you?"

"I don't know." She gave a slight shrug. "My driver's license says I live in Denver. Surely I'm used to snow. This can't be my first blizzard."

"But it's the first one you remember."

She let out a slow breath. "That's it exactly. I don't remember being in a blizzard before. I sure don't remember hearing the wind howl like this. At least with the TV on, I couldn't hear it so much. Maybe…"

"Maybe?"

"Maybe we could talk so I won't think about it."

"Sure. If you want. About what?"

"Tell me about Belinda."

When he smiled, it lit up his eyes. "Belinda? She's a pistol."

"You like her."

"Yeah. I like her."

"What's she look like?"

"Hmm. Well, she's about five foot four, wears her hair real short. It's black, so she fits in with the rest of us around here," he added with a tug on the hair above his ear.

"It's hard to believe I saw her just a few hours ago and have no memory of it. Of her."

Jack shook his head. "You didn't see her. You must have stopped at the house and picked up that envelope—there's no postage or mailing address on it, so she didn't mail it to you. But she and Ace weren't there. They left three days ago for a belated first anniversary in Hawaii."

"Their first wedding anniversary? In Hawaii. That sounds romantic. Palm trees, sandy beeches, luaus."

"Have you ever been?"

"No, I— Oh, you're sneaky. I answered without even thinking."

"But you know you've never been to Hawaii."

She tilted her head and thought about it. "No, I've never been." She smiled. "Another piece of the puzzle. I know I've never been to Hawaii."

They were quiet for a few minutes, watching the fire. Then Lisa said, "Tell me more about Belinda."

"I don't know what you want to know. She's pretty, has big gray eyes, and Trey calls her The Fox." He chuckled. "When Ace isn't looking."

"Ace is her husband?"

"Yeah. My oldest brother. Trey's our youngest brother."

"Wait a minute. How many brothers do you have?"

"Just the two, Ace and Trey."

A wide grin spread across Lisa's face. "Ace, Jack, and Trey? Don't tell me. Your sister's name is Queen."

Jack let out a much-used groan. "It would've been if the old man had had his way. But her mother put her foot down. They compromised on Rachel, which is the name of the queen of Diamonds.''

"You're kidding. The queen of Diamonds has a name?''

"All the face cards have names, but don't ask me what they are.''

Jack could see that the conversation was keeping her mind off the storm. He was glad it was so simple to diffuse the tension he'd sensed in her. She was easy to talk to and seemed genuinely interested in what he had to say. What man wouldn't be flattered? So he kept talking.

Lisa was grateful. As long as she could watch the play of firelight over the chiseled planes and hollows of his face as he spoke, and listen to the sound of his deep voice, she didn't have to think about the fact that she couldn't remember. She could ignore the storm, the snow, the lack of electricity—and the likelihood that the situation in which she currently found herself might not improve for days.

So she asked Jack questions, encouraged him to talk. He told her about his family's ancestor, a young baron from England, who, nearly penniless, had come to America to make his fortune. He'd ended up in a poker game in Cheyenne, where he'd gambled everything he had on the deed to a Wyoming ranch. He'd won on a bluff. The only card of any significance in his hand had been an ace.

"So the ranch wasn't named after your brother?''

"No, it's been the Flying Ace since 1880-something.''

"Tell me about your family.''

"You don't want to hear all that.''

"Oh, but I do," she said. "Families fascinate me. I always wanted one."

Jack cocked his head. "You did?"

Lisa frowned. "I don't know why I said that. It just came out."

"You're starting to remember."

"How sad," she said with a smile that matched her words, "that the one thing I can remember about myself is that I never had a family. I don't remember it, really, I just…feel it."

No, that wasn't quite right, either, she thought. She didn't feel it, but she remembered the feelings. And that made no sense whatsoever. She could remember the longing, the terrible deep yearning for a family of her own. Yet here and now, stranded in this house with the fire blazing and the wind beating against the windows, she didn't feel that yearning, that longing. She no longer even felt the tension that had plagued her since she'd realized she'd lost her memory.

No, sitting there and listening to Jack's deep voice as he spoke of ancestors, poker games and a ranch called the Flying Ace, she felt peace. And that feeling felt…new. As if she hadn't known much peace in her life.

"You're tired," Jack observed.

She gave him a wan smile. "I guess I am. I should go to bed."

Jack shook his head and stood. "The bed'll come to you. By morning that bedroom will be cold."

"You're going to move the bed in here?" She sat up straighter on the couch. "Don't be silly. I can sleep on the couch. Oh, but then where would you sleep, right?"

"I can sleep anywhere," he said. "You're the one

who's sleeping for two. I'll bring the mattress in here and put it in front of the fire. You pick the place—mattress or couch—where you're most comfortable.''

His idea was so logical that Lisa decided they would both be better off if she helped him rather than argued.

In the bedroom she held the flashlight while Jack stripped the bed. She'd forgotten about the cash she'd stashed beneath the mattress. At the first good tug on the sheets, stacks of it came flying out.

''What the hell?'' Jack muttered.

Lisa was too stricken to say anything. Shocked, because she'd forgotten the money. Confused because she couldn't imagine any legitimate reason for a person to be carrying that much cash. Guilty because she feared she may have stolen it.

Jack shook his head. ''Since I seriously doubt Belinda was quite that thorough when she stocked the house, I have to assume the money is yours. What are you doing stuffing it under the mattress? What a cliché. Not that we're likely to be seeing any burglars around here, but if we had one, this would probably be the first place he'd look. Come on, give me the flashlight so I can— Ah, hell,'' he said when he saw the look on her face. ''You were hiding it from me. You don't know me from Adam. You were worried I might steal it.''

''No,'' she protested. ''No. I was afraid that if you saw it you might think I'd stolen it.''

The idea that this beautiful woman with the wounded look in her eyes could steal money was so ludicrous to Jack that he burst out laughing.

Lisa bristled. She had worried herself sick over that

money when she'd found it, and now he was laughing. "What's so funny?"

"The thought of you," he said, his laugh trailing off to a chuckle, "as a hardened criminal."

Fear trailed up her spine. "But what if I am?"

She wasn't kidding, Jack thought. It was there in her eyes, the dismay, the fear that she might have done something wrong. He shook his head. "In the first place, if you were the type to steal money, you probably wouldn't be so worried about it after the fact."

"How can you say that?"

"Look at you. You're appalled at the very *idea* of stealing. That alone should tell you that you'd never do such a thing."

"You can't know that," she said with a little hitch in her voice.

"All right, then try this. I know Belinda. She would never be friends with anyone with criminal tendencies."

"Maybe she doesn't know me as well as she thinks she does."

"Yeah, right," he said with a snort. He reached to take the flashlight from her so he could collect the cash that was now scattered all over the floor, but her hand was clenched around the casing like a vice. "Give me the flashlight," he told her. "I'll pick all this up and you can stash it in a drawer or somewhere."

"You're being awfully casual about this," she told him, her voice wavering.

"Why are you so eager to believe the worst about yourself?" Jack frowned. "Maybe I'm wrong. If you really think you stole the money, maybe that's your subconscious talking to you. Maybe it's telling you it's true.''

Lisa felt her stomach wind itself into a tight greasy knot. ''Maybe it is.''

Jack shook his head. ''No, I just can't see it. What would you have done? Waddled up to the bank teller, waved a gun in her face, then waddled back out through the lobby?''

He was making fun of her. She didn't know whether to be hurt, insulted or charmed. ''I do not waddle.''

He took the flashlight from her grasp and started around the bed collecting twenties and hundreds into loose piles. ''You obviously haven't seen yourself walk lately.'' Over his shoulder, he tossed her a wink. ''You waddle, Ms. Hampton. You waddle.''

The money was once again stashed in the black bag in which Lisa had found it that afternoon. The bag was tucked into the bottom drawer of the dresser in the bedroom.

Jack had carried the mattress into the living room and put it on the floor before the fire. Together he and Lisa had spread the sheets and two blankets over it, then Jack had dragged the couch up next to it, directly across from the fire.

The couch formed a wall, of sorts, a barrier to help trap the heat and reflect it back over the mattress. It would help avoid Lisa's roasting on one side and freezing on the other.

Every minute or so she rolled over, shifted, bunched her pillow.

Maybe it wasn't working, Jack thought. ''Are you comfortable down there?'' he asked from where he lay stretched out on the couch. "Are you too hot, too cold? Or maybe hot on one side and cold on the other?"

"No," she told him. "The temperature's fine."

"I can bring in the box spring to put under the mattress if it's too hard there on the floor."

"There's no need for that. It's fine, Jack. Thank you for asking, though." Lying on her back near the fire, Lisa rolled her head on the pillow and looked at him. "What about you?"

"Fine." The couch was about six inches too short, but he'd get over it. It was cooler this far away from the fire. He wanted her closer to stay warm. He wanted her to be able to stretch out, turn over if she wanted. And he damn sure didn't want to worry through the night about her falling off the couch.

"You're sure?" she asked.

"I'm sure." What he was sure of, more sure every second, was that she didn't want to go to sleep. They'd been bedded down for nearly an hour and she had yet to settle. "What's wrong?"

"Nothing."

"Come on. Out with it. Are you sick? Does your head hurt?"

Lisa bit the inside of her bottom lip. Obviously she wasn't fooling him. Particularly not when her restlessness was keeping him awake. "No, nothing like that. I'm sorry. I just...I'm afraid to go to sleep."

He raised himself on one elbow and propped his head on his hand to look at her. "Why?"

"It's silly, really. I'm afraid that when I wake up I may not even remember what's happened since you found me in the car. I told you it was silly."

"I don't know. In your place I might be thinking

the same thing. But you know that won't happen. You've got a concussion, that's all.''

"I know. I guess.''

Jack waited, and when she didn't say anything else, he began to relax. He was dog-tired and wanted nothing more than a few hours of sleep. A six-inches-too-short couch, no matter how cushy, wasn't as comfortable as the bed up in the cabin, where he'd just spent four days and nights of coveted solitude, but he was too tired to care.

"Jack?"

Hell. Didn't women ever run out of things to say? "Are you asleep?"

He thought about letting out a snore for an answer, but he couldn't do it. She was scared, and he didn't really blame her. Besides, she already knew his eyes were open. They were open because his gaze was drawn to the way her hands lay curved protectively over the baby in her womb.

What did that feel like? he wondered. To create brand-new life, to carry the miracle of creation inside your own body and feel it there, feel it grow and come to life.

What did it feel like for a man to know that his love for a woman had created that new life? Did the baby's father have any idea how lucky he was to have such a caring woman carry his child?

"No," he said quietly, meeting her gaze, telling himself it wasn't any of his business to wonder where the man was, to want to throttle him for letting her take off alone into the back of beyond in the winter in Wyoming, for pity's sake. "I'm awake."

Lisa had been scrambling frantically for something to ask him to keep him talking. Maybe if he talked long enough, that deep voice of his would sooth the edges of her raw nerves and she could sleep. She was physically tired. Exhausted. But her mind, holes and all, refused to shut down.

Then something Jack had said earlier triggered a question. "When you were telling me why your sister wasn't named Queen, you said something about *her* mother."

"Yeah?"

He sounded irritated that she'd asked. "I'm sorry. It's none of my business."

Jack let out a breath and flopped back down to stare at the ceiling. "It's no big deal. Hell, you must be the only person in the county—half the state, maybe—who doesn't know that my mother was a barmaid over in Cheyenne."

"That's a tough job," Lisa offered. "A hard way to make a living."

"Would have been, if she'd been trying to make a living. She was more interested in catching some rich man's eye."

Lisa smiled dreamily, spinning a story in her head. "I don't know about the rich part, but she obviously caught your father's eye."

"Yeah. It was just her dumb luck that he already had a wife."

"Oh." The fairy tale in her head burst and disappeared. "I'm sorry. That must have been difficult for her, raising a child on her own. Difficult for you, growing up without a father. Unless...did she ever marry?"

Jack snorted in disgust. "I doubt marriage was ever in her plans. She just wanted some rich man to take care of her until she found the next, richer, man. But she knew even before I came along that King Wilder wasn't that man.''

''But you ended up with him eventually, didn't you? I mean, your name is Wilder, and I take it this was his ranch.''

''Yeah, it was his, and I ended up here. She died when I was twelve. Her sister didn't want anything to do with me. Can't say I blame her much for that—I was more than a handful, and I meant less than nothing to her. So she brought me to the man she said was my father. Dropped me on the doorstep. Literally. You should have seen the look on his face.''

Lisa would have had to have been deaf not to hear the bitterness in Jack's voice. Her heart ached for the boy he had once been, lost, unloved, unwanted. She felt a deep empathy and wondered, because of the strength of it, if her own life had been similar.

But something good must have come of those events in Jack's early life, because he had a family now and spoke of them with affection, with love.

''Your father didn't know about you?''

Jack's brief laugh was hard and dark. ''Took him completely by surprise. Him, and his wife. And their three kids. It was an interesting day, the day I showed up, any way you look at it.''

''It must have been terrible for you,'' she said softly.

''It was no picnic, that's for sure. Not for any of us. Except maybe King. After the initial shock wore off, he was too busy proudly proclaiming he had another son to worry about much of anything.''

''So he wanted you?''

''He wanted another Wilder trophy. I fit the bill.''

"I can't imagine how difficult that must have been for you to be thrust into that situation."

"I think it was harder on them. Ace was fifteen, and suddenly here's this twelve-year-old punk being forced on him." He chuckled. "God, how we fought."

"What about your other brother, Trey?"

"He was only seven, and he resented the hell out of me. But he was too little for me to beat up on, so it was mainly me and Ace. Didn't last long, though, only a few months."

"You came to terms with each other?"

"We didn't have much choice. Rachel put her foot down."

"Your sister?"

"Mm-hm. She was barely five. A little angel, I remember thinking. She told Ace and Trey that I was just as much her brother as they were so they had to be nice to me, and that was that."

"That's sweet."

"Rachel's a gem, all right. She even got Betty to try to be nice to me."

"Betty?"

"Her mother. King's wife. She's the one my existence hurt the most."

"I can imagine."

"No," he said quietly. "You can't. The whole reason King went to Cheyenne all those years ago and spent the weekend with my mother was because the Wilders' two-day-old son, their second son, had just died. King couldn't handle it, so he figured getting drunk and making it with a barmaid would take his mind off his troubles."

"Nice man, your father."

"Nice woman, my mother. The dead baby's name was Jack. I figure my mother chose my name nine months later deliberately."

Lisa sucked in a sharp painful breath. "I'm sorry, Jack. So sorry. I shouldn't have pried."

"If it still bothered me, I wouldn't have said anything. Don't worry about it. Try and get some sleep."

"All right. Good night."

"Night."

Lisa rolled toward the fire to toast her front for a while and bit her tongue on any more questions. It wasn't fair of her to pry into Jack's life, particularly when he couldn't pry right back into hers.

She wondered what, if anything, she would have told him, had she had any memories upon which to draw. Was she an outgoing person whose life was an open book? Or was she private? Maybe even secretive?

Beneath her hand the baby stirred.

Whatever and whoever Lisa was, she was about to become a mother. She closed her eyes and smiled.

"Jack?"

"Hmm?"

"I don't waddle."

Jack got up twice during the night to add wood to the fire. Each time, he knelt on the mattress and woke Lisa. If that hit to her head was hard enough to cause amnesia, he worried about what other effects it might bring on. The possibilities gnawed at him. Dizziness, blurred vision. Coma.

Each time he woke her she was progressively crankier. Lucid, still with no more of her memory than when she'd first come to out in the car. And cranky.

Damn his hide. He shouldn't think cranky was cute.

Each time after replenishing the fire and waking her, he'd gone back to the couch and told himself he was a fool. The moaning wind seemed to agree with him.

One time he had looked out the blinds and seen the blowing snow, so the next morning he wasn't particularly surprised to find the blizzard still raging.

He wasn't one damn bit happy about it, but he wasn't surprised. And he was kicking himself for picking this particular week to take off for the mountains. With Ace gone, and Frank, their horse trainer, off to see his grandkids in Provo, that left only Stoney and Trey to haul hay out to the cattle.

But hell, they couldn't even do that until the damn storm quit. If Jack was home, all he'd be able to do was pace the floor and wait with them for the weather to clear. Worry with them over how many cattle they might lose.

Instead, he was here and they were there, probably worried about him. Not that either would admit it, to him or to each other. Trey would grumble and curse him for being gone when he was needed. Stoney, the foreman who had taught them all how to run a ranch when their parents died and who was now retired from that job but still working for the Flying Ace, would tell Trey not to worry. After all, hadn't Stoney taught Jack everything he knew? "He'll be fine. Mark my words," Stoney would tell Trey.

Still, Jack was feeling guilty for not being there when he knew he was needed. He would just have to make sure he got there as soon as he could.

Being as quiet as possible so he wouldn't wake Lisa, Jack added more wood to the fire, then carried his boots into the kitchen before putting them on.

He'd watched her during the night. Watched her sleep. He'd never done that before, watched a woman sleep. It wasn't something he was going to be in a hurry to do again. It had done funny things to his chest, making everything in there feel tight.

On the other hand, he didn't think he'd ever seen anything more beautiful than Lisa sleeping, with her cheeks flushed, her lips pouty, her hand curved protectively over her unborn child.

Beautiful.

But that was beside the point. He had no business watching her sleep, no business thinking about some of the things he was missing in life. He didn't need a wife of his own, or children. He had his family— brothers, sister, nephews.

He'd thought about a family of his own before. Had taken it as far as convincing himself he was in love with Marsha. He'd asked her to marry him.

She'd turned him down. What a kick in the teeth that had been. She said he didn't love her enough. She wasn't important enough to him.

The hell of it was, she'd been right. He'd liked her, cared about her, had a lot of affection for her, and in bed they'd been great together. But he knew that if he had looked in the mirror he would never have seen that goofy dopey look on his face that he'd seen on Ace's every time big brother thought about Belinda.

Marsha had also said that with his past, he had no firsthand knowledge of what it took to be a good father, so how could he be one himself?

Jack tugged on a boot and resisted the urge to

stomp his foot into it. No sense waking Lisa just because Marsha had hit the nail smack on the head.

And no sense watching Lisa sleep again, either. Somewhere out there a man was surely wondering where she was, when she was coming home. A man who loved her.

And if there was one thing Jack Wilder was not, it was a poacher.

Anyway, he didn't figure he had it in him to love a woman the way a woman deserved to be loved. If he did, he figured he'd have tumbled by now, be married by now. But he didn't, he hadn't, and he wasn't, so that was that. She would need a good father for her baby, too. Marsha had been right about him on that—he wasn't good father material, wouldn't know the first thing about how to raise a kid.

He tugged on his other boot, then thought of coffee. God, he wanted a cup.

The electricity was still off. No surprise there. Depending on the nature of this particular outage, it could come back on any minute, or, if ice had weighed down the power lines so much that they had snapped somewhere miles from town, the power could be off for days.

That being the case, he gave the automatic coffeemaker a sorrowful glance and pulled out the small dented coffeepot from his saddlebag. Thank God the stove in this house was gas.

By the time he had the coffee on, it was light outside. He bundled up in his coat and gloves, gritted his teeth, tugged his hat on tight and stepped out into the blizzard to see about his horse. By the time he got back, if he didn't freeze solid and fall over and get buried in a snowdrift on the way, the coffee should be just about right.

Chapter Four

The sound of the back door closing woke her. Lisa sat up with a start. "Jack?"

He didn't answer. But then, she'd known he wouldn't. She knew, simply by the feel of the air in the house, that she was alone.

He'd left her.

"Don't be a ninny." She tugged her slippers on and struggled to her feet. He'd only gone out to check on his horse, to feed it, make sure it had water. He hadn't left her here alone, hadn't abandoned her.

And why, she wondered as she tugged on her robe and rushed into the kitchen, would she think he'd abandoned her? Was that a common fear of hers, being abandoned? What an unsettling thought. She was a grown woman, about to become a mother. She might even be some man's wife, although she wore no wedding ring. She was an adult. She made her own life, didn't she?

Yet the more she thought about it, the more certain she became that that sudden sharp fear of having been abandoned was an old fear, one she had known intimately.

Who had abandoned her? Her parents? Her baby's father?

She told herself it was the draft of cold air in the kitchen that made her shudder, not the almost-memory that teased her before disappearing back into that black void that was her past.

"Stop it," she told herself. "Stop looking for trouble. There's enough right here and now to deal with."

The top half of the back door held five diamond-shaped panes of glass. Lisa looked out to discover a screened porch, with waist-high stacks of firewood along two sides. The screen, all the way around, was packed with snow. She couldn't see a thing through it.

She moved to the window over the sink, which looked out on the side yard, and caught a glimpse of a dark shape—Jack. He was only about twenty yards from the house, with snow nearly to his knees, and he was already disappearing into blowing blinding snow.

If it was her out there, she'd surely get lost. But she had to assume Jack knew where he was going. That he knew exactly where the barn was. That he wouldn't get lost in the blizzard.

He was bound to be frozen by the time he got back. She turned toward the stove and saw the pot of coffee there on the front burner. Now that she'd seen it, the smell made her mouth water. The same coffee can she'd seen yesterday now sat on the counter beside the stove.

Decaf. Lisa's knees weakened in gratitude. She'd never been worth a damn without a cup of coffee first thing in the morning. If it had been regular coffee she wouldn't have been able to drink it. Caffeine was bad for the baby.

No wonder Belinda was her best friend.

Lisa paused. Without realizing it, she had just uncovered another piece of herself. She wasn't worth a damn without her morning coffee—decaf or not.

With a wide smile—she'd remembered something about herself!—she rushed to the bathroom, then to the bedroom to get dressed. Jack was going to need something more substantial than a cup of coffee, but Lisa didn't intend to get caught at the stove in her gown and robe.

A few minutes later she was dressed and stirring a pot of oatmeal on the stove when Jack stomped the snow off his boots out on the porch, then came in.

The utterly domestic scene wasn't new to Jack. Countless times he had walked into a kitchen to find a woman at a stove. And like now, it had always been someone else's woman. His stepmother. His brother's wife. Aunt Mary. The housekeeper.

But whichever woman it had been at any time, she hadn't been there cooking for him. She'd been cooking for the family and hands. For the ranch. It had never been personal.

But this time it felt personal. This woman made him want it to be personal. And he resented that wanting. His life was just fine the way it was. He didn't need a woman in it, didn't want one.

She turned, a big spoon in her hand, her cheeks

flushed, her eyes bright. "I know how to cook oatmeal, and how to make toast in the broiler."

She looked so pleased with herself Jack couldn't help but smile. "Sounds good," he said. This wasn't personal. She was just cooking oatmeal. Nothing personal in that.

She looked like a cupcake, all round and sweet. And wasn't that a hell of a thing to think about a woman!

"But if I ever made coffee on a stove before, I don't remember it. How do you know when it's ready?"

"I'll take care of it." He unbuttoned his coat and hung it on a peg beside the door, then tugged off his boots and set them below his coat.

"Oh, look at you!" she cried. "You're freezing to death, and here I am going on about knowing how to cook oatmeal." She put down her spoon and rushed toward him. She cupped her hands over his icy cheeks.

For a moment Jack couldn't move. He'd come in the door irritated with himself, then she'd somehow managed to delight him. Now he couldn't think of a word to describe what he felt as she stood there pressing her hands to his face. He wanted to close his eyes and sink into her touch. Just sink right in to the warmth of her palms, their softness, their strength. Had a woman ever touched him this way before? Had a woman ever seen the coldness he felt inside and offered to warm him with her own flesh?

Never. Not like this.

Lisa wasn't even aware how profound this moment was for him. And Jack planned to keep it that way. He smiled and stepped back. "I'm fine. Really."

"You're sure?" she asked.

"I'm sure."

Together they put breakfast on the table. While they ate, Jack fiddled with the battery-powered boom box, trying to find any news about the storm. Such as when it might abate. All he could get was an oldies-rock station. Everything else was static. He left it on the oldies station in hopes there would be a weather update soon.

"I have a cell phone in my purse," she offered. "But I tried it and it says there's no service."

"The signal doesn't hit this area. We're below a ridge."

When they finished eating, Jack heated water on the stove for washing dishes. As they did the night before, he washed, Lisa dried. On the radio Anne Murray was asking if she could have this dance for the rest of her life.

Listening to the dreamy waltz, Lisa shook water from Jack's coffee mug and started drying it. "I wonder if I know how to dance."

Jack's response came without thought. Quickly drying his hands, he turned and took the cup and towel from her and said, "Let's find out." He placed her left hand on his shoulder and took her right in his. "Don't think."

"What?"

He led her off in the simple one-two-three of the slow waltz. "Don't think about it. Don't wonder if you know how."

He had already distracted her enough with those few words that she wasn't thinking, wasn't wondering if she knew how to dance. She was following his lead. She was dancing.

A slow smile spread across Jack's face. ''There you go. I'd say you've danced before.''

It didn't matter that the hand that held hers was rough with calluses, or that he was in his socks and she in her slippers, or that there was more static than tune coming from the radio. Lisa was in heaven. Her smile was at least as wide as his. ''I know how to dance.''

Then, without thinking, she began humming the melody.

Jack took it slow and easy, with small steps at first, but as confidence bloomed across her face, he altered his steps until he was turning in one spot, whirling her around him. To him, her laughter was better than any music.

He was just slowing her down as the song came to an end when she hit a wet spot on the floor and slipped. Before the small cry had even left her mouth, Jack caught her. His arms slipped around her and pulled her flush against him.

''Oh.'' She looked up at him, startled.

''I've got you.''

But the minute Jack spoke the words, he wondered who had whom. Yes, he had his arms around her and was holding her, but she had him, too, with those big green eyes, that soft lush mouth that tempted him to taste, to feel. To take.

He'd been celibate too long. That was the only explanation for why she was affecting him so strongly.

Bullhockey, bud.

The truth was, she was a beautiful alluring woman. It just stunned him that he could be so attracted to her when she was so pregnant. Not that her being pregnant took anything away from her beauty, her allure. But Jack had a deep and abiding respect and reverence for life, and for any female of any species who carried that life inside her. He'd never been sexually attracted to a pregnant woman before. It was a new experience and not a little unsettling.

He wasn't going to kiss her. Her hands were on his shoulders, his arms around her rib cage. Her face was close to his, her lips unconsciously inviting. But he wasn't going to kiss her.

Lisa's breath caught. He wasn't going to kiss her. Surely he wasn't. And surely she didn't want him to. Too many unanswered questions weighed on her mind. She didn't need this kind of temptation. Didn't want it. She could not, absolutely could not, be physically attracted to him. He was practically a stranger. She was mega-pregnant and might be married.

Raging hormones. Didn't pregnancy cause hormone levels to fluctuate? That was all this was. Of course it was.

And he couldn't really want to kiss her, anyway. There was nothing the least bit enticing about a woman whose belly stuck out to there.

That belly, or rather, the baby inside it, settled the matter by giving Lisa a strong kick.

Jack felt it right through his belt. Startled, he looked down to where her abdomen pressed against him. "Whoa."

"Oh," Lisa said on a breath. She stepped back from Jack and covered her abdomen with both hands. "Oh…" With her hands cradling her womb, she closed her eyes and tilted back her head. The miracle of life moved beneath her touch. She knew she had felt it before, but she couldn't exactly remember it. This was, for all practical purposes, the first time she'd felt her baby move. And suddenly she had the overwhelming urge, the *need* to share it.

Without thought, she looked up at Jack, took his hand in hers and placed it on her stomach. "Feel."

Jack wanted to pull away, step back, avoid this. Touching her this way seemed too...intimate. It wasn't his place to be the man she shared this with. He knew that. Yet something held him there. Maybe it was the look in her eyes, the plea that begged him to let her share this with someone. And he was the only one there.

Then he felt it, a slight movement at first, then a definite little jab. And he was lost. "God," he whispered in awe. "I felt it. Lisa..." Something deep inside Jack Wilder was forever changed. For as long as he lived, no matter whom she was married to, this woman and her child would be a part of him.

Lisa's eyes were glazed with moisture. "She likes you."

Jack swallowed hard. "She?"

Lisa smiled at him. "She. It's a girl."

A girl. God, a baby girl. Right there beneath his hand. He felt like a man who had never been around imminent birth before. As if the miracle of life and birth didn't go on around him as regularly as clock-work. Just then, none of that meant anything. This was Lisa's baby. This was special.

A girl, she'd said. "Does this mean you're starting to remember?"

Lisa shook her head and her smile faded. "No, it's not like that. I mean, I guess maybe *remember* is the wrong word. It's just that...it's familiar."

Suddenly feeling like a fool as well as an interloper, Jack took his hand from her belly and stepped back. "What about her father?"

Lisa's jaw hardened. Fire sparked in her eyes. "She may never know she has one if the jerk doesn't back off."

"Lisa?"

"Oh, my God. Why would I say something like that? What does it mean?" With her arms wrapped tightly around her belly and her shoulders hunched, she looked up at Jack with such confusion and devastation that something deep inside him ached for her.

"You don't remember?"

Lisa forced herself to think. Think hard. "I don't..." It was there, she knew it was. The answer was there in her mind...but the harder she tried to grasp it, the more elusive it became. Pain shot through her temple. She squeezed her eyes shut and pressed the heel of her hand against the pain in a futile effort to ease it.

"Lisa?"

"I can't grasp it. It's there, but...then it's not. It hurts!" she cried. "God, it hurts."

"Lisa, stop." He pressed his hand over the one she held against her head. "Ease off. Don't think, just relax. Take a deep breath."

She couldn't think, couldn't move. By rote she followed his soft-voiced instruction and inhaled deeply.

"That's it. Now let it out."

She exhaled.

"Again. Slow and easy," he crooned. "That's it, just slow and easy. Don't try to force it."

As he continued to talk, to comfort her with his deep voice, Lisa felt her tension gradually ease.

"Okay," she said. "I'm okay."

"Look at me." Jack waited until she raised her gaze and he could look directly into her eyes and judge for himself. "All right."

"It's not all right," she countered.

"You said you were okay."

"I am," she said. "The situation isn't. Why would I say something like that about the father of my baby?"

Jack shrugged and urged her toward the living room. As they passed the end of the kitchen counter, he reached out and turned off the radio, cutting off what had become in the past few minutes nothing more than nerve-racking static.

"It was probably something simple," he said, "like maybe he left his dirty socks in the middle of the floor."

The idea that she might have run all the way from Denver to Wyoming with her medical records and more than seven thousand dollars in cash to stay in the middle of nowhere by herself simply because a man left his dirty socks lying around was so absurd that Lisa burst out laughing.

"Hey, husbands have been known to do stuff like that."

The word *husbands* gave Lisa pause. She searched her mind, her heart. Did she have a husband? Was she married? Did she love the man who'd fathered her child?

Nothing. There was nothing there but emptiness. How could she forget such a thing as a husband?

She looked down at her hands and frowned. "I don't have a wedding ring."

Jack guided her around the mattress on the floor and over to the couch. "You know that doesn't mean anything. A lot of married people don't wear wedding rings.''

''I would.'' Somehow she knew that. ''I would want that visible symbol.'' She looked up at Jack. ''I don't feel married.''

''That's your amnesia talking,'' Jack said. ''But it doesn't really matter right now, anyway, does it? It'll all sort itself out once your memory returns.''

Would it, Lisa wondered. Would it really?

As a distraction, Louis L'Amour turned out to be a good one. Jack had dug out the three slim paperbacks from his saddlebags, and Lisa, who had never read a western, had to be dragged away from her second one so she could eat the sliced-turkey sandwiches Jack had made for lunch.

''It'll still be there after you eat,'' he told her.

''But they're just about ready to—''

Jack rolled his eyes. ''I've created a monster.''

''No,'' she said with a laugh. ''Just a new Louis L'Amour fan.''

An hour after supper they ran out of reading material. Jack broke out his deck of cards.

''Good grief,'' Lisa said with a laugh. ''What else do you have in those saddlebags?''

God, he loved hearing her laugh. ''Nothing much.'' He didn't know when he'd ever felt so lighthearted. ''Just my dirty socks.''

He wanted to kick himself the minute the words were out of his mouth and he saw the light in her eyes dim. He'd just reminded her of a couple of the million questions that haunted her—who and where was her baby's father.

"So," she said after a long moment, "what are we going to play?"

Okay, he thought. If she could carry on and act as if he hadn't just stuck both boots in his mouth, so could he. "Ever play five-card stud?"

"You mean poker?"

Jack paused. Was that look of blank innocence on her face for real, or was it just a bit too casual? "Yeah," he said cautiously. "I mean poker."

She flipped her hands in the air. "I have no idea. I guess we'll find out, won't we?"

They found out. But only after they determined what they would play for. There were no matchsticks or toothpicks to be found in the house. Jack had no money on him at all.

"All we need is some loose change," Lisa said.

"I just spent three days alone in the mountains. There was no need to take any money, change or otherwise. Nowhere to spend it."

Lisa nodded her understanding.

"That settles it, then." Jack gave her an exaggerated leer and wiggled his eyebrows. "We'll have to play strip poker."

"Oh, yeah, right." The idea was so ludicrous and his expression so comical that Lisa burst out laughing. "Like anyone would want to see this misshapen body." Then, ignoring the odd look that crossed Jack's face, she straightened and said, "I've got money."

Slowly his expression cleared. "Your stash?"

"Whatever you want to call it." Lisa figured that if it was her money, she was certainly within her rights to use it to play poker. If it wasn't her money, well, it would all go back in the bag when they finished playing, anyway. It wasn't as if they were going to wear it out or anything.

So they divided the money in half and settled on the mattress before the fire. Jack explained the rules, the different hands, what beat what, while Lisa nodded and took notes.

"You're writing it down?" Jack nearly laughed at the idea.

"How else am I supposed to remember everything?"

He shrugged. She had a point. He definitely had her at a disadvantage. Which, in poker, was the whole idea.

And wasn't it cute? he thought with a secret smile, watching her look at her cards, then refer repeatedly to her notes. When she won the first hand, he felt like a proud papa.

"This is fun," she decided as she raked in her winnings. "Can we play again?"

"I'm counting on it." He gathered the cards and handed her the deck. "Your deal."

During the course of the next few hours, she took him for every one of his thirty-five-hundred-plus dollars.

It took Jack a long time to go to sleep that night. He was used to long days filled with hard physical work, but for the past several days he'd done nothing more strenuous than carry a feather-light woman from her car to the house.

That same woman lay only a few feet from where he lay on the couch. She was curled up, facing away from him toward the fire.

Watching her sleep was keeping him awake. After

the fire burned down enough that he could add more wood, he turned his back to the room, and the woman.

It didn't help. He might not be able to see her, but he still knew she was there. He could still think about her. About sitting across the breakfast table from her. Sharing the mundane chore of washing dishes. Dancing with her.

God, he shouldn't have done that. Shouldn't have held her in his arms. Shouldn't have been holding her when the baby kicked. Shouldn't have let her press his hand there so he could feel it.

Damn, he was never going to fall asleep at this rate.

But he must have, for the next thing he knew, he was awakened by a high keening moan.

Lisa.

Jack rolled from the couch and landed on his hands and knees beside her on the mattress. She was moaning and rolling back and forth in agony, the blanket a tangle around her legs.

"Lisa, what is it?" Visions of premature babies stopped the breath in his lungs. "What's wrong?"

Her face was a grimace of pain. *"Cramp."*

"Oh, God, honey." More than alarmed, he pulled the blanket away from her and reached beneath her down-stretched arms to gently spread his hands across her abdomen. "Easy does it."

But she wasn't having any of his *easy*. She thrashed back and forth, eyes scrunched shut, breath hissing between her teeth.

"Lisa, honey, baby, you've got to be still and let me feel. You're going to hurt yourself. You might hurt the baby."

"I already hurt," she managed in a tight voice. "But it's not the baby, it's my foot."

"Your what?"

"My foot, my foot."

Was the pain making her delirious, or was she out of her mind with panic? "What about your foot?"

"I have a cramp in my foot."

Jack figured that later he might think back on this event and feel like a fool. But for now he was just so damned relieved she wasn't going into premature labor that he wanted to laugh in sheer relief. A cramp in the foot—that he could deal with.

And he did. Now that he knew what was wrong, he realized she was trying to grab her right foot, but was having trouble reaching over her stomach to get to it. He took the foot in his hand and stretched the cramping muscle by pulling her heel down toward him and pushing her toes toward her knee.

It was such a small foot, dainty and delicate. Pale in his weather-darkened hand. Soft as a baby's behind against his rough calluses. While he pushed her toes up to stretch the muscles in her arch, he smoothed his thumb along the curve to help ease the ache.

After a long moment Lisa let out another whimper, this one of relief.

"Better?"

"Oh, yes," she said with a sigh. "Thank you."

Jack knew that if she could see over the mound of her stomach she would realize that in all her thrashing around, her nightgown had worked its way around and up until it barely covered the tops of her thighs. He wasn't about to tell her. There was no point in causing her any embarrassment. But as he gave her arch a final massage, it was all he could do to keep from staring at that expanse of pale creamy flesh.

Mercy, she had great legs, long and lean and curved in all the right places with feminine muscles.

One more deep rub with his thumb along her arch, and he placed her foot gently on the mattress and pulled the blanket up to her waist.

"You scared ten years off my life," he admitted with a crooked grin. "I thought you were going into premature labor."

Lisa closed her eyes and stroked her stomach. "Don't even say it. Besides," she added with a soft smile, "this little girl wouldn't do anything so rude as to arrive early."

"Let's hear it for polite little girls," he said fervently.

A moment later Jack was back on the couch, knowing he wouldn't sleep for the rest of the night. Visions of long legs and a soft smile would keep him awake.

Chapter Five

The radio declared the blizzard to be the worst in fifty years. Jack didn't doubt it. The storm stretched from southern Canada clear down into northern New Mexico, and according to all reports, showed no signs of letting up soon.

It was late afternoon, two full days since the blizzard had started, before the wind finally died.

At first Lisa didn't realize the significance of the silence. She was dozing on the couch when she slowly became aware that something was different. She blinked her eyes open and sat up, looking around the living room, trying to decide what that difference was.

She could hear Jack shuffling cards at the kitchen table. She could hear the fire crackling quietly in the fireplace. She could hear...absolutely nothing else.

"Jack," she called, pushing herself up from the couch and rushing to the kitchen.

Jack heard her and dropped his cards. "Lisa?" He jumped to his feet, the chair scraping loudly across the floor. He started toward the living room. "What's wrong?"

They met each other where the kitchen met the living room.

"Jack, listen," she said intensely.

"What? Are you all right? I don't hear anything."

"The wind stopped."

By damn, she was right. "Finally."

He went to the back door and stepped out onto the screened-in porch. Lisa followed him. Because of the snow still packed against the screen, they couldn't see out. He pushed open the screen door. A large clump of snow was dislodged and fell to the snow-covered ground.

Beyond the door, the landscape looked like a fairy-tale wonderland. Drifts curved elegantly, as if sculpted by a master artist. Dips and hollows added contrast, while giant perfect snowflakes floated lazily from the sky. The path Jack had forged to and from the barn was no more than a shallow dip, but still visible.

"Oh," Lisa breathed. "It's so beautiful."

"It is." There was at least two feet of snow, with some of the drifts more than four, maybe five feet in places. Jack forced away worries about how many cattle had died in all this beauty. It ate a hole in his gut, but there wasn't a damn thing he could do about it just then, and there was no point spoiling Lisa's pleasure. Watching the delight on her face was putting another very different type of hole in his gut.

"If I had a pair of boots," Lisa declared, "I'd be out there right now making snow angels and catching snowflakes on my tongue."

"As high as some of those drifts are," Jack teased, "you'd need boots up to your armpits."

"Are you trying to tell me my slippers and loafers won't do?"

Jack shook his head and laughed. "I'm still trying to figure out why a person would come to Wyoming in the middle of a blizzard without bringing along a pair of boots."

"According to the radio—and you—this blizzard was a complete surprise. Besides, my feet have been so swollen for the past few weeks that my loafers are the only shoes I can get into."

When Jack merely grinned at her, she frowned. "What?"

"You did it again. Remembered something."

"I don't—"

"You remembered that your feet have been swollen."

She made a face. "The sad state of my feet is more than obvious. Even if I can't see them most of the time," she added ruefully.

"True, but just because they're swollen now doesn't mean they've been that way for weeks—yet that's what you said. You remembered it."

She sighed and looked back out at the falling snow. "For all the good it does me. I still can't go out there."

The look of yearning on her face was so intense he could practically feel it. She'd been cooped up in the house for two full days, not even sticking her nose out the door until now. How was he supposed to resist when he had the power to safely grant her wish to go outside? "Sure you can," he heard himself say.

Within a very few minutes they were both bundled up in their coats. The only gloves Lisa had were thin kid-leather driving gloves, but they would have to do. Jack made her put on her thickest socks and her loafers. She found a pair of earmuffs in her coat pocket and put them on.

Then Jack scooped her up in his arms and carried her out into the snow. He had to check on Skeezer anyway, and he figured it wouldn't hurt Lisa to get a little fresh air. The barn was close, the wind had died and the temperature felt as though it hovered somewhere just barely below freezing. As long as she stayed dry and warm and wasn't out for more than a few minutes, she would be fine.

When he swept her up in his arms, Lisa shrieked with delight. "I think I'm going to start calling you Sir Jack."

"How's that?"

"This is the second time you've rescued me. The first time from my car, this time from cabin fever." She settled in his embrace and, feeling perfectly at home there, wrapped an arm around his neck. "My very own personal knight."

No one had ever called him a knight before. Jack kind of liked the sound of it. It was nonsense, of course, but he still liked it.

He carried her through the snow toward the barn, placing each foot carefully so as not to slip. The Coleman lantern, held by the bail in his left hand, banged gently against his thigh.

Lisa threw back her head, face to the sky, and laughed for the sheer pleasure of it. "This is wonderful." With her mouth open, she stuck out her tongue to catch the icy flakes. "Snow ice cream," she declared. "That's what we need, snow ice cream. Oh, but I bet Belinda didn't stock any vanilla. Surely she wasn't that thorough."

"I doubt it, but we'll look when we go back."

Still holding her, Jack managed to get the barn door open. Once inside he put her down on her feet and quickly closed the door. It wasn't warm inside, by any means, but Skeezer gave off a great deal of heat, so it wasn't as cold as it was outside.

But it was dark. He lit the lantern while Skeezer nickered a greeting.

Lisa didn't know if she'd ever been in a barn before, but despite an air of abandonment—it was empty but for Jack's horse—she liked the smell. And she liked the way the horse looked at her, as if eager for her attention.

"Hello, fella," Lisa said softly. "He is a fella, isn't he?"

"Mostly. He's a gelding."

Lisa approached the stall where the horse stood with his sturdy neck arched over the stall door. "What's his name?"

"Skeezer. If you scratch him behind his ears, he'll be your friend for life."

"Is that so, Skeezer boy?" He was so big, Lisa thought, both enchanted and leery. "Will you let me scratch behind your ears? I think I could use a friend for life."

In response the horse nickered again.

"Well, then, you're going to have to bend down here to me, because I'm not as tall as Jack. I can't reach your ears."

As if understanding her and deciding to play, the horse lowered his head and butted her gently in the chest.

Lisa stumbled backward with a startled laugh that was part nerves, part delight.

"Easy, boy." Jack was there instantly to make sure Lisa didn't fall. "She's not some ol' cowhand you can knock around like that. You have to be gentle with her."

"I'm all right," Lisa protested. "He just surprised me, that's all."

Jack made a low humming noise and took Lisa's gloved hand in his. Together they reached up and stroked the horse's jaw. That was all it took for the big animal to lower his head and tilt it until their hands, which hadn't moved, were just behind his ear. Letting out a *whoosh* of breath, Skeezer moved his head slightly up and down.

Lisa laughed. "He's petting himself."

"He'll do this all day if you let him."

Jack stayed there for several minutes, assuring himself that Lisa was all right. He didn't ask, because he figured she didn't remember one way or another, but he assumed she hadn't been around horses much.

While she scratched behind the gelding's ears, Jack took the bucket out to the well house and used the hand pump to fill it. When he got back, he cleaned out Skeezer's stall and put out more hay and a little grain, then placed the bucket of water in the corner of the stall.

"Ready?" Jack asked Lisa a few minutes later.

Since Skeezer had abandoned her in favor of the grain Jack had put out, Lisa reluctantly nodded.

Jack turned off the lantern. He didn't want to carry it lit while he had Lisa in his arms.

"Now that the blizzard has stopped," Lisa asked, "do you think anyone will come looking for us?"

"Nobody's going to come looking for me. As far as anybody knows, I'm snowed in up at the cabin. But if anybody knows you're here, they might start plowing the road, even with this much snow still coming down."

Lisa let out a sigh. She didn't know how she felt about being rescued, and that troubled her. Maybe if she knew why she had come to this isolated house in the first place, she might be able to decide if she *wanted* to be rescued.

When the hiss from the lantern was finally silent, Jack said, "Here we go," and scooped her up in his arms again. He acted as though her weight was of no consequence.

"After all this lifting, I'm going to have to find something really hearty to feed you for supper to rebuild your strength."

Jack snorted. "You don't weigh as much as a feather pillow."

"You've got to be kidding. I'm as fat as a pig."

"You're not fat, you're pregnant." He squatted to grab the lantern in his left hand, letting the weight of her legs rest in the crook of his left elbow.

"I can carry that," she offered.

"I've got it."

She released a dramatic sigh. "Yes, Sir Jack."

Jack chuckled and let them out of the barn, closing the door securely behind them. They were about halfway to the house when Lisa began shifting in his arms.

Jack stopped. "What's wrong?"

She arched her back and made a funny face. "I'm fine. It's just that someone is poking a foot in my ribs."

He smiled in sympathy. "From the inside, huh?"

"Yeah."

Jack started off again, walking carefully through snow that came halfway to his knees in the places he'd already walked and above his knees when he stepped in fresh snow. It was hard to judge where to step when he couldn't watch his feet.

Suddenly Lisa gasped and arched again, throwing his balance off just enough that he knew what was going to happen but couldn't do a thing to stop it. All he could do was twist sideways so that he fell backward into a big soft drift, with Lisa still cradled in his arms, the lantern still clamped in his hand.

He landed halfway between sitting and lying, with Lisa's weight knocking a soft "umph" out of him. Snow caved in on them, falling in their faces.

Startled, Lisa shrieked. To Jack's disgruntled ears it sounded like laughter.

Lisa sputtered and wiped snow from her face. She looked at Jack and burst out laughing. "Are you all right?" she managed.

Slowly he reached up with one gloved hand and pushed the snow off his face to reveal a frown of disgust. "I was going to ask you that same question, but I have to figure that if you can laugh like that while my butt's buried in snow..."

"I'm sorry." She howled with laughter again. "You should have seen the look on your face when your feet went out from under you."

"You know," he said, raising a snow-covered

brow, "it's really not wise to make fun of a man who has all this snowball-making material at his disposal."

"Same goes, Mr. Wilder, for men who threaten women who not only have access to that same material, but who aren't being held down by a whale and are therefore freer to move around." Her left arm was still behind Jack's neck, but while she spoke, she had a devilish gleam in her eye, and her right hand kept sifting through the snow, bringing up a handful and letting it drift down again.

Jack's eyes narrowed. "You wouldn't."

"Is that a dare?"

"It's more like a plea. The last time I got in a snowball fight I was outnumbered three to one. At my age, defeat is humiliating."

Lisa chuckled and brushed a clump of snow from his forehead. "Who beat you—your brothers?"

"Worse. My nephews."

At the sight of the smile that lit his face, something inside Lisa shifted. She was afraid it might be her heart. Had she ever met a man like him? He was so kind and strong and honorable, so thoughtful. He was fun to be with. He made her laugh and wasn't afraid to laugh at himself. And he was so…masculine. Rugged. As if he could withstand anything the world might throw at him and shrug it off.

Oh, Lisa, this isn't smart.

No, she thought, hearing that warning voice in her head, this wasn't smart. She shouldn't be caring so much about a man she barely knew.

On the other hand, she thought with chagrin, he was, for right now, the only man on the face of the planet she did know.

But it wasn't smart to feel these things about him when her life was a mess and her memory nonexistent. Good heavens, if she wasn't mistaken, she was, at this very moment, on the verge of leaning over and kissing him. How could she be so drawn to him when she couldn't even remember her baby's father? Was she fickle? A woman of loose morals? Did she have no sense of honor?

And how, she wondered, did a woman this pregnant, with no memory at all, cope with these sexual stirrings? Stirrings for a stranger.

"How about a truce?" she offered quickly. She had to get away from him, had to put some distance between them and keep it there.

"A truce sounds fine with me," Jack said. He wondered what thoughts were going through her mind to make her blush and look away like that. Or maybe it was just the cold stinging her cheeks that made them look so rosy.

Funny, but he couldn't remember ever having so much trouble taking his gaze off a woman before, or taking his arms from around one to let her go. He didn't want to let this woman go.

The truth settled over him as lightly as the snow falling from the sky. She was important to him, this woman with no memory. She tugged at something deep inside him he hadn't known was there and couldn't name.

He couldn't love her; he didn't have it in him to bare his emotions to a woman. But he could take care of her, help her, watch out for her. She was too vulnerable right now, physically because of the baby she carried, emotionally and mentally because of her memory loss. She needed looking after. If, in the end, he had to hand her back to a husband or lover, so be it. That was the best thing for her, anyway. She needed a man who could give himself to her, and that man was not Jack Wilder. She wasn't his for the keeping, only for the care he could give her for a little while.

"Come on," he said, shifting his feet for better purchase in the snow. "Let's get you back to the house before you catch a chill."

Lisa huddled before the fire trying to get warm. It wasn't so much the cold she'd brought in with her from outside that kept her shivering as it was the realization of just how much Jack had come to mean to her in such a short time.

Where was her common sense? What had happened to that warning she'd issued to herself when she first met him that reminded her that men were not to be trusted, that they were only nice when they wanted something? She'd trusted Jack from the beginning, and look where it had gotten her, with these odd yearnings to feel his lips on hers, to cuddle in his arms, to see his smile, hear his laugh.

Lisa, Lisa, get a grip.

She was worrying for nothing. Her hormones were fluctuating, that was all. As for Jack, he was just a nice man trying to make the best of an awkward situation.

She prayed that her baby's father was as nice a man as Jack. Yet that one troubling thought she'd had from out of nowhere—a thought she'd expressed—that her child would never know the father if the man didn't back off, ate at her. What did it mean? Had she left him? Was she hiding from him? Was he abusive or just a jerk? If he was either of those things, why in the world had she let him close enough to get her pregnant?

God, the questions were tormenting her. She wanted answers. She wanted her memory back.

Soon, she promised herself. Surely soon.

The blizzard had stopped. With any luck, they'd be able to get out of here tomorrow and she could...what? Where would she go? What would she do? She didn't know a single person on earth beyond Jack.

The stark reality of that thought sent another shiver racing down her spine.

From the corner of her eye she saw him come and stand in the doorway. "There's a bathtub filled with hot water with your name on it, if you're interested."

Her mind had been a million miles away; it took a moment for his words to register. Even when they did, they made no sense. "What hot water?"

At his small smile, she knew what he had done. She'd heard him clanking around in the kitchen but hadn't paid any attention. He'd said he had to clean the snow out of the lantern, take it apart, dry it off. She'd thought that was all he'd been up to.

But now she recalled he'd also been making several trips into the bathroom. She could see the bright glow of the lantern spilling from the bathroom doorway just around the corner in the hall. He'd been heating water on the stove and carrying it into the bathroom. Quite a bit of water, if the tub was hot, as he'd said. He'd done it so she could have a hot bath. If that wasn't the sweetest thing anyone had ever done for her...

"Oh, Jack..."

"Go on, before it cools off. But don't pull the plug when you're finished. I'll take my turn after you."

As much as she wanted to linger, to lie back and soak in the water until her fingers and toes wrinkled, Lisa hurried through her bath so the water would still be at least warm for Jack. When she left the bathroom, she was still so confused about her growing feelings for him, her reaction to him that afternoon in the snow, that for the first time she felt shy around him. She ducked her head and told him it was his turn, then made a beeline for the mattress before the fire.

When Jack came out of the bathroom a short time later, he found her curled on her side facing the fire, her eyes closed. But she wasn't asleep. She was gripping the top edge of the covers so tightly her knuckles were white.

He started to ask her what was wrong, but swallowed the words. It didn't take a rocket scientist to know she'd read his mind that afternoon when they'd fallen into the snow and she'd ended up on his lap. Surely his wanting her had been plain on his face.

No wonder she didn't want to look at him. No wonder she didn't want to talk.

He didn't care if the snow stopped or not. Tomorrow they were out of here. He couldn't take another day and night alone with her. She made him want too many things. Things he knew would never be his.

Chapter Six

Sometime during the night the snow finally stopped. The sky was cloudless, and at dawn the sun was a winter-yellow ball rising out of the snow.

"What happens now?" Lisa asked, stirring her oatmeal to help it cool. They were the first words either of them had spoken since they'd awoken. "Since the snow's stopped, will someone come after us, do you think?"

"Maybe, but there's no sense in waiting around to find out."

"You mean we'll leave? How?"

"I'll ride to headquarters and come back in the truck."

Lisa looked down quickly in hopes he wouldn't see the sudden panic in her eyes. He was going to leave her here? Alone?

Be careful what you wish for.

She had wanted more distance between them. She was about to get more than she'd hoped for.

But this was for the best, wasn't it? She was in danger of becoming entirely too reliant on Jack. Was she the type of woman who needed a man to lean on, to do for her, take care of her? Lord, she hoped not. She much preferred to think of herself as a strong independent woman who could stand on her own.

It didn't seem as though she was very independent or strong if the thought of being left alone for a few hours could panic her. She had thought it before, and it seemed now to be true. Lisa Hampton was something of a wimp.

But she didn't have to be. She wouldn't be. Squaring her shoulders, she looked across the table at Jack. "There's no need for you to hurry on my account. I imagine you'll have plenty to do once you get home."

Jack eyed her carefully. "What do you mean?"

Striving for a casualness she didn't feel, Lisa gave a shrug. "I mean that I don't see any reason for you to have to come all this way back to get me. I obviously came here on purpose, with the intent of staying by myself for a while. There's no reason I can't stay here and do as planned."

"With no electricity? No water? No phone? No way."

"Are any of those things likely to be working at the ranch headquarters?"

"Maybe, maybe not," he said. "But if you think I'm leaving a pregnant woman out here alone in these conditions, you're out of your mind."

She hadn't counted on his getting angry, hadn't considered that he would. But he was, there was no mistake about it. Those dark blue eyes were shooting sparks at her. A muscle in his jaw flexed, and his lips thinned to a hard line.

Lisa searched inside herself but found no fear of him. Instead, she found fascination. Not because of his anger, but because it was a side of him she'd not seen before.

When she didn't argue with him, Jack visibly relaxed. It seemed to take him some effort. Then he said more easily, "If that's not good enough for you, how about hot and cold running water?"

"Won't the electricity be out there?"

"It might, but we have a generator for the well."

Oh, my, she thought, so much for independence. Besides, as much as she hated to admit it, he was right. She should be thinking about her baby and making sure she didn't put herself in a position to do it harm. Even if she had electricity and running water, she did not have transportation. Deliberately trapping herself here, with no means to get to a doctor if anything went wrong, was just plain foolish.

She gave him a nod of capitulation. "I'll be packed by the time you get back."

It didn't take Jack as long as he'd estimated to get back to Lisa. When he'd left her, he'd taken the road because it was safer for the horse. There were gullies and washes around the section house that he knew would be filled with snow, impossible to detect until it was too late. He wouldn't risk Skeezer breaking a leg just to shave half a mile or so off the ride.

About a mile before he would have reached headquarters, he ran into Stoney, who was in the process of plowing the road.

"Where ya headed?" Jack asked when they met.

"Got us a city gal, friend of Belinda's, stayin' out at the section house," Stoney told him. "If she ain't froze to death by now. Figured I better get out there and check on her, bring her back to the house."

"You figured right." Jack told him what had happened, then the two men traded places. Stoney rode Skeezer back to headquarters while Jack climbed into the rig and plowed his way back to Lisa. The county would plow the highway and other county roads, but private ranch roads were left to the ranchers. Every winter the Flying Ace attached a plow blade to the front of every rig to keep the ranch roads passable.

As he started slowly down the road, Jack glanced in the rearview mirror and watched Stoney ride back toward headquarters. Stoney had known Lisa was here, said he'd met her the day she arrived. He was shocked to learn about her accident and her memory loss, but he didn't know anything about her except that she was Belinda's friend.

Other than having her identity confirmed, Jack had learned nothing.

His eagerness to get back to her worried him. It wasn't for her sake, to get her to the house, where she would be more comfortable, that he was so eager. He just didn't like being away from her. And that scared the hell out of him.

It was midafternoon by the time Jack got Lisa settled into Ace and Belinda's house. The electricity was already back on there, although it would probably be another few days before it was on at the section house.

He gave her a quick tour and showed her where everything was, then he had to get to work.

Trey and Stoney had been out most of the day checking on the herd. It didn't matter how much grass was under all that snow; a cow would stand and starve to death rather than paw the snow aside the way a horse would. So the men hauled hay and prayed they wouldn't find any dead cattle. They always found at least a few after a storm this bad, but they prayed, anyway.

By the time the three men made it back to headquarters and compared notes, it was nearly dark. Among them they'd counted ninety-three head dead, most of them yearlings. It could have been worse, much worse, but this was bad enough. They would probably find more when the snow melted.

Exhausted, each man made his way home. Trey had his own house on the north side of the ranch so he could be close to his wheat and alfalfa fields. Stoney lived in the bunkhouse and was eager to settle in front of his television, now that the power was back on, and watch that night's episode of *Nova* on PBS.

Jack lived in the foreman's house, about a quarter of a mile from the main house. When he'd first come to the Flying Ace, Stoney, of course, had lived there.

When King and Betty Wilder had been killed on the ice-slicked highway coming home from Jackson Hole the winter Jack was seventeen, it had been Stoney who'd held them all together while twenty-year-old Ace got his feet under himself and took control of the ranch. It had been Stoney who'd taught all four Wilders everything they needed to know to stand on their own and keep the Flying Ace prospering.

As far as Jack was concerned, Stoney Hamilton *was* the Flying Ace. Jack, Ace, Trey and Rachel had been shaken the day eight years ago when Stoney had announced his retirement. He'd looked Ace in the eye and said, "If even half of everything I've taught you has sunk in, you'll make Jack the new foreman. He's the man for it now."

For as long as he lived, Jack would never forget that day. The sadness at the thought of Stoney's putting himself out to pasture because he was getting too old to do the job. The pride that the old man thought Jack could handle it. The fear of trying to step into the boots of the man who'd been more of a father to him than his own father had.

They'd tried to talk Stoney into staying in the foreman's house. Hell, it had been built for him; he'd done most of the work himself.

But Stoney had insisted he was tired of living by himself. He would move into the bunkhouse. He wasn't leaving the ranch. There was still plenty he could do around the place, plenty he could teach the youngsters, as he called anyone under fifty.

So Stoney had moved into the bunkhouse. Jack had been living in the foreman's house now for years. He liked it, liked his privacy. But tonight when Jack stepped into his house, it felt different. It felt…empty. Lonely.

He told himself it wasn't because he missed Lisa. He didn't miss her. Didn't miss her smile, her laughter, that sudden softening in her eyes whenever she felt the baby move. Didn't miss her sweet feminine smell or those crazy yellow slippers.

No, it wasn't his house that felt empty, it was the ranch itself, without Ace and Belinda and the boys. That was it.

When did you start lying to yourself, pard?

All right, dammit. He missed Lisa. He was worried

about her being alone the whole day in a strange house with no one to talk to. He couldn't help it. It was the caretaker in him.

When he passed through his kitchen, he spotted a note taped to the table. It was from Belinda, telling him that her best friend, Lisa, was staying at the section house and asking Jack to keep an eye on her and make sure she had everything she needed.

Hell. What Lisa needed was her memory, and there didn't seem to be anything Jack could do about that.

At the bottom of the note, Belinda had left the phone number of the resort where she and Ace were staying. Without trying to talk himself out of it, he picked up the phone and dialed.

He got the voice mail for their room.

He didn't want to leave some cryptic message that he wouldn't be able to explain in the short amount of time the machine allowed, so he hung up. He would try again later.

He showered and shaved and put on clean clothes. He would go to the main house and tell Lisa there was nothing to eat in his kitchen and he'd come to mooch a meal.

Sounded good to him.

Lisa vowed she would never take such things as central heat, electric lights, hot and cold running water or toilets that flushed for granted again.

That wasn't to say she wouldn't seriously consider trading all of them away if it meant having Jack with her again.

"Don't be ridiculous," she muttered to herself as she finished unpacking in the guest room. She was perfectly fine on her own. If she was the type of woman who needed a man to make her happy, she wouldn't have come to Wyoming alone to stay in an isolated house.

She did feel a fondness for that little house, though. This one was much larger and nicer, with two stories and a basement. In addition to water and electricity, she had a washer and dryer, a microwave and a working phone.

But this home belonged to a family who would be back soon. Lisa felt like an interloper, as though she should tiptoe through the rooms lest she disturb someone. Which was ridiculous, because there was no one there to disturb.

When she finished unpacking, she carried her dirty clothes down to the laundry room in the basement. While they washed, she wandered the rooms on the main floor, staying out of the private areas, such as the housekeeper's room off the kitchen and the office off the living room. That left the large kitchen, formal dining room and living room. It was odd how much a person could tell about a family just from those three rooms.

The old chrome-legged table in the spotless kitchen seated ten, and the floor was worn beneath the chairs. They ate here often, together. Family was important to them. The high chair in the corner was old and made of wood, and spoke of new beginnings, of continuity, as if this wasn't the first generation of Wilder children to use it. But there were recipe boxes piled on the seat, and a wooden bowl of wax fruit sat on the tray. The children had outgrown the high chair, but it wasn't put away. Perhaps it waited for the next baby.

Lisa stroked her belly and wondered if back in

Denver, at the address on her driver's license, a high chair waited for her child to be born and grow big enough to sit in it. She wished she knew. She wished she had a large loving family like the one she sensed lived in this house. But surely she didn't have a family, or at least not much of one, or she wouldn't be here in Wyoming alone, separated from them, with a baby on the way.

In the formal dining room the gleaming table was made of maple and seated a dozen. The walls were lined with portraits and photographs of what she assumed were past and present generations of Wilders. Big rugged men, women who looked deceptively dainty and delicate—until you looked in their eyes and saw the strength and determination.

It hurt to look at all those family members and believe that she had no family of her own. She turned away from the wall of portraits and wandered into the living room.

This room, too, shouted *family,* with the ragged teddy bear on the long sofa, the bucket of plastic horses beside the big-screen television. Side by side on the coffee table lay two magazines, one about quarter horses, the other about the Internet. The incongruity made Lisa smile.

If she had to invade this home, she could at least make certain it was as clean when the Wilders returned as it had been when they left. Not that it was dirty, but they'd been gone for several days, and a light coating of dust had settled over the furniture. She would ask Jack when they were due back and make sure it was clean by then.

That was assuming, of course, that she saw Jack again. He hadn't said anything about it when he'd left her here. He hadn't said much about anything other than to show her where things were in the house.

Naturally he would have a lot on his mind. There was a ranch to manage, cattle to check on. Lisa had no idea what those duties involved, but she was sure it was a great deal of work.

There was a knock on the back door. Then the door opened and Jack called, "Lisa?"

Something warm and tingly swept through her. "Jack!" She was halfway across the kitchen when he crossed the mudroom and stepped into the kitchen doorway.

Jack stopped and stared in awe. A thousand times or more he'd come through this doorway and seen first his father, then later, Ace, being greeted this way by a woman. Jack had looked on indulgently and thought it was nice.

He'd had no idea what it could do to a man, to have a woman rush toward him this way with a smile in her eyes, her cheeks flushed, his name on her lips. Men had killed for less important things. Had died for them.

He'd been wrong. It wasn't *nice*. It was…shattering. Because it wasn't his, and he'd suddenly discovered that he wanted it to be. He wanted, badly, to come home at the end of another brutal day and find a warm smiling woman—*his* woman—waiting for him. She would greet him with a kiss and he would take her to his bed—*their* bed—where they would make sweet hot love, then fall asleep wrapped in each other's arms.

He'd never done that before, slept all night with a woman. He'd never awakened in that cold dark hour before dawn to warmth and softness. And he wanted to. Standing there now looking at Lisa, with her beautiful face, her body bulging with the miracle of new life, he wanted it all. The woman. This woman. With a child on the way. A family.

"Jack?" Her smile faded. "Is something wrong?"

Jack mentally shook himself. "No." Hell of a daydream, but that was all it could be. If he wanted a woman to love him, he would have to love her back, and he'd had the ability to love anyone other than his brothers and sister burned out of him a lifetime ago. No way was he going to offer himself to some woman only to be scornfully rejected. No way in hell.

"Are you sure?" she asked, her face slipping into a frown.

"Yeah," he said firmly, "I'm sure." He tugged off his coat and hung it on a hook on the wall of the mudroom, then jammed one heel into the bootjack beside the door. "I just couldn't find anything to eat at my place. There's usually plenty of food up here."

Together they searched the pantry and freezer and found that Jack was right—there was more than enough food for a good-size army. Seeing all the food available made Lisa smile.

"Something funny?" he asked.

"No." She took two cans of beef stew from a shelf in the pantry. "But seeing all of this tells me I can cook something other than oatmeal."

"You remember how to cook?"

She shrugged and carried the cans to the counter. "I just know that I know how to cook. In fact, I think I love to cook." She proved it during the next few minutes by grinning the entire time she mixed together the ingredients for corn bread without having to look for a recipe.

"A day or so ago you mentioned other men here," she said as Jack set the table. "What are they doing about supper?"

"Stoney's eating at the bunkhouse and Trey went home."

"Trey's your younger brother, right?"

"Right."

"He doesn't live here on the ranch?"

"He does, but he lives on the north side so he can be near his crops. Trey's the farmer in the family."

"There's no reason for him or Stoney or anyone else to have to cook after working all day. I'd be glad to cook for them."

"Are you sure? Shouldn't you be taking it easy?"

"I'm sure," she said. "If I take it any easier, I'll be in a coma. I'll thaw a roast for tomorrow night."

Jack nodded. "All right, but supper only. I might come up and rummage around for something to eat for lunch now and then, but half the time I take something out with me so I don't have to come back."

"What about breakfast?"

"No way," he protested. "You're not getting up at five in the morning just to cook for the rest of us."

"I wouldn't mind. Honestly."

"I would. We will not be here for breakfast. End of discussion."

She gave him a mock salute. "Yes, sir."

His lips quirked. "Good enough, then."

While the stew heated and the corn bread baked, Jack reached for the phone on the wall beside the back door. "I'm going to call and check on the boys."

"Your nephews? Where are they?"

"They're at my sister's. Donna, Belinda's housekeeper, took them up there to stay with Rachel and Grady's five-year-old, Cody, while Ace and Belinda are gone.''

Lisa didn't actually eavesdrop, but she couldn't help overhearing Jack talk with his sister, then each of his nephews. His love and genuine affection for them came through clearly in his voice and on his face, as he asked each boy in turn about his day, did he get to play in the snow, was he minding Aunt Rachel and Donna, was he behaving in school, was he having fun.

She wondered if his nephews knew how lucky they were to have such a large loving family.

The roast the next night was a big hit with Stoney, Trey and Jack. Almost as big a hit as Lisa herself.

Trey shook his head, marveling at her. ''My hat's off to you,'' he said. ''If I had to walk around not knowing who I was or anything about myself, you'd have to lock me in a padded cell. I'd go crazy.''

Lisa liked Trey. She liked Stoney, too, but it would have been impossible for her not to like Trey, who looked, spoke and acted so much like Jack. The family resemblance was unmistakable. Trey had that same black hair, those same dark blue eyes, the same rugged features.

She smiled at him. ''It's pretty frustrating to recognize all the advertising jingles on television when your own name sounds foreign to you.''

Trey shook his head again. ''All that, and she can cook, too. I vote we keep her.''

Lisa laughed, as she knew was expected, but she couldn't keep her gaze from shooting to Jack. She couldn't keep the blood from rushing to her cheeks.

She couldn't keep her heart from whispering, *Yes, keep me, Jack.*

She jerked her gaze away. She couldn't believe that thought had even crossed her mind!

Mind? What mind? She'd obviously lost hers when she lost her memory. She had to stop these crazy yearnings for Jack. She had a baby on the way, a life to recover, if she could. She couldn't handle any more complications, and if ever there was anything on earth designed to complicate matters, it was the human male.

Oh, good grief. There it was again, that negative attitude toward men. Her past history with the opposite sex must be dismal indeed if such cautions survived her memory loss.

"Go on with ya," Stoney said. "Look, you've embarrassed the poor thing." He reached across the table and patted Lisa's hand. "Don't you pay him no never mind, Miss Lisa. What he meant to say was that if you'd a mind to stay, we'd sure enough find a place for you, and that's a fact. And not just 'cause you can cook. Why, we'd be happy just to look at your pretty face every day."

Jack jabbed his fork into a chunk of roast on the platter and moved it to his plate. If anything, Lisa's face was redder now than before. "Sure glad you didn't wanna embarrass her," he said to Stoney.

This time when Lisa laughed, Stoney's face was as red as hers.

"Well," Stoney said, "she can cook if she wants." Then his twinkling eyes narrowed on Lisa. "As long as you don't cook up any of that sissy food."

"Sissy food?"

"Fancy stuff, like shrimp casserole or something."

Lisa crossed her heart and held up her hand. "No shrimp casserole. Got it."

"Did anybody check the highway today?" Jack asked, changing the subject after the round of laughter.

"I did," Trey said, "when I drove out to the mailbox. Road's clear, as long as the wind doesn't pick up and blow snow all over it again. You needing to get to town?"

When Jack answered Trey, his gaze was on Lisa. "I need to haul Lisa's car in so she won't be stranded out here."

Lisa started to object. Jack had too much work to do already, what with the snow and the cattle and all. But the truth was, she would feel a whole lot better if she had a car at her disposal.

"How bad is it?" Trey asked.

"I didn't get a good look, but I'm betting the radiator's busted."

Lisa winced. That sounded costly. But what the heck. She had all that cash, and her car had to be repaired. Later tonight she would check her wallet again for an insurance card. Surely she had insurance. Maybe it would help pay for the repairs if they were very expensive.

"Thank you, Jack. I hadn't even thought about how I would get it fixed."

When supper was over and the others left, Jack lingered. "There's another reason I want to go to town tomorrow," he told her. "I'd like to take you in and let a doctor look you over."

Once more Lisa wanted to object, but she couldn't. He was right. She needed to see a doctor to make certain her accident hadn't harmed the baby. And maybe a doctor could tell her if and when her memory might return.

Please, God, let it be soon.

She gave Jack a smile of thanks. "My car and I will be grateful to be hauled to town and checked over."

The next morning Jack hooked up the tow bar to the back of his rig, and he and Stoney drove to the section house and hauled Lisa's car out of the ditch and over to ranch headquarters. The radiator was definitely shot.

Back at the house Stoney climbed out of Jack's rig and Lisa got in, and they drove to Hope Springs, the only town in Wyatt County.

They stopped first at Curly's Auto Garage and left her car. Curly promised to call the ranch no later than the next day and let them know a cost and time estimate on the repairs.

From there Jack took Lisa to the hospital. He stood in the waiting room and watched as Lisa, with her medical records in hand, disappeared into an exam room.

He was still there an hour later when she came out.

"What did he say?" he demanded as he held out her coat for her.

Lisa slipped her arms into the sleeves, then turned and beamed at Jack. "Dr. Carver says the baby is fine. No apparent ill effects from the accident."

Jack nodded. "You can trust him. Will's a good doctor. What about you?"

"I'm not a good doctor at all," she deadpanned.

"Very funny." He tweaked her nose.

Lisa laughed. "I'm okay. I've suffered a mild concussion, which accounts for my memory loss. He says this is pretty rare, but not unheard of. I'm not supposed to try to force any memories. He says it won't help. I have to let them come back on their own."

Jack slipped on his own coat, then placed his hand at the small of her back and guided her out the door into the bright cold sunshine. "Are you all right with that?"

"I'm trying to be," she said. "I might as well be, since there's nothing anybody can do about it."

"It's way past lunchtime. How about something to eat?"

Lisa blinked, then laughed. "Until you said that I hadn't realized I was hungry, but now I'm starved."

"Then let's eat."

Lisa had seen the sign at the edge of town stating that the population of Hope Springs was an even 2,022 people. She hadn't realized how small that was until they drove from the hospital at the edge of town to the café in the center of town on Main Street. The entire trip took three minutes. During that short drive, several people waved or honked at Jack, and he waved back.

"Do you know everyone in town?" she asked, teasing.

"Pretty much."

Oh, my. He wasn't teasing, he was serious. He really did know just about everyone in Hope Springs. Lisa wondered why she found that endearing.

Harvey's Café was sandwiched between a dry cleaner and a video-rental store. When they entered, a bell jingled above the door. Jack helped her off with her coat, then hung it and his, along with his hat, on the coat tree provided. He led her to the front corner booth, and within seconds a waitress appeared with ice water and menus.

"Hey, Jack, how's it going?"

"Fair, Arlene. How about you?"

"Countin' the days till my vacation."

"How soon do you leave?"

"Seven months and twenty-three days."

Jack laughed. "Eager to go, are you?"

"What gave you that idea? Can I bring you some coffee? Tea?"

"I'll have coffee. Lisa?"

"Do you have decaf?"

"Sure do. I'll be right back."

Jack looked across the table to find Lisa smiling at him. "What?" he asked.

"You really do know everyone in town, don't you?"

"It's not hard. There aren't all that many people to know."

Jack didn't need to look at the menu. He was having the day's special—roast beef, mashed potatoes and gravy, and green beans.

That sounded like more than Lisa wanted to eat, so she opened her menu to see what else was available. She began to smile.

"See something that looks good?" Jack asked, curious about her smile.

"Actually it all looks good, but I just realized that I have one more piece of information about myself that I can file away."

"What's that?"

"I love Mexican food."

When Arlene returned with their coffee, Jack ordered the special, Lisa the enchilada platter. When the food arrived, Lisa leaned over her plate, closed her eyes and inhaled the fragrant steam rising from the spicy food.

"Oh, yeah," she said with feeling. "This is going to be great."

While they ate, Jack told her about the time he and Arlene had met. Arlene was a couple of years younger than Jack, but she had a brother Jack's age. They were in high school, attending a football game, and her brother, Ken, had been giving her a rough time about dating a guy from Pinedale in the next county. Arlene had gotten fed up and went to punch Ken in the nose, but Ken had ducked and she'd hit Jack, instead.

The way Jack told the story had Lisa laughing so hard she had to hold her sides.

Then he pointed out one person and then another on the street and told funny stories about them. Once he even winked at her.

In that moment Lisa doubted she'd ever been happier. Despite the frustration of her memory loss, things couldn't have been better. Her baby was healthy, the sun was shining, and Jack Wilder was flirting with her.

Oh, she knew he didn't mean it, but that was all right. Today didn't count. It was a day out of time, a day for pretending that, for now, everything was wonderful.

So she flirted right back.

Across the room at a little table by the hall that led to the rest rooms, a stranger watched and smiled. Finally he'd found her.

It was no effort to hear their conversation. The guy

told the waitress that Lisa was staying at the ranch. The four-wheeler they'd pulled up in sported a logo on the side for the Flying Ace ranch.

The man who'd hired him to find the woman would be pleased.

Well, scratch that. Nothing pleased the man who'd hired him. But the news of the woman's whereabouts would be welcome.

The stranger paid his bill, then went out and sat in his car to place the call on his cell phone.

Chapter Seven

By the time they pulled up to the back door of the house it was dark, and Jack was having a little problem with reality. His mind kept slipping back to that tantalizing fantasy he'd been having since the day he'd carried Lisa in from the cold.

The bad part was, the fantasy didn't seem as terrifying now as it had the first few times he'd had it. Why should it scare him to imagine that this was all real? That Lisa was his. That he'd taken her into town for a prenatal checkup. That they'd spent the day together. That he'd taken her out for a late lunch so she wouldn't have to cook once they got home.

Most of it was true. There was no harm in altering the facts a little. It was a private thing, existing only in his mind. What could it hurt to pretend?

Next, if this was real and not just his imagination,

he would take her inside and carry her to his bed. *Their* bed.

"Oh, Jack, thank you."

It took him a full minute to realize that Lisa had actually spoken, that he wasn't making it up. He blinked the vision away and put the truck into park. "What are you thanking me for?"

"For today. It was wonderful."

When she leaned toward him across the seat, Jack held his breath. She tilted her head and aimed a kiss at his cheek.

He didn't know what made him do it. He must have lost his mind. At least his willpower. Definitely his common sense. At the last possible second, just before that enticing mouth would have brushed his cheek, he turned his head. Toward her.

Lisa saw the move too late. For one stunning second her lips brushed his. Heat and electricity sparked from the contact.

Startled, shaken, Lisa sucked in a breath and pulled back. She froze a fraction of an inch away. If she so much as pursed her lips, she'd be kissing him. If she leaned forward just the tiniest bit...

Oh, how she wanted to lean forward, purse her lips, kiss him. How she wanted him to kiss her back. The wanting was so strong and yet so foreign, as though she'd never known such a thing before, that she jerked away, shaken.

Heaven help her, he looked...disappointed. As if he'd wanted them to kiss. After all, he was the one who moved his head, turning her simple gesture of thanks into something that could have been much more.

Lisa's heart raced. He had wanted to kiss her. *Her,*

a woman nearly eight months pregnant with another man's child.

But when she met his gaze, she couldn't deny what she saw there, and what she saw was the look of a man who wanted to kiss a woman.

"Jack—"

"I'm sorry." He turned his gaze away and stared out the windshield. "I didn't mean to offend you."

If her laughter sounded as though it was more from shaky nerves than humor, Lisa couldn't help it. "I felt a number of things just now, but *offended* isn't even on the list."

Jack looked at her. With one finger he tucked her hair behind her ear. "You're too honest for your own good, you know that? You could give a man ideas. And that's not smart."

"No." She huffed out a breath. "It's not smart, is it." She made it a statement rather than a question. "Can we…just forget it?"

"No," he said quietly. "But…"

"But we won't let it happen again," she finished for him.

"That'd be best."

"Yes." She shrugged. "Roger always said I wasn't any good at…at this man-woman stuff, anyway."

Beside her, Jack stiffened. "Roger?"

Lisa shuddered. She couldn't believe the words that had just come from her mouth.

"Who's Roger?" Jack asked.

"I…" She pressed her fingertips to the dull throb in her temple. "I don't know. It was there, then it was gone. Damn!" she cried. "Why did I say that?"

"Easy," Jack crooned, pulling her hand away from

her head. "Just take it easy. Remember what the doctor said about not trying to force it."

"I can't stand this," she said. "Why would I say that?"

Jack was furious, and trying to hold it in. How dare some bastard say a thing like that to her. Jack would like to get the jerk alone in a room for five minutes and teach him some manners.

But Lisa didn't need his anger right now; she needed reassurance. "It's the sort of thing a weak man says to a strong woman. He tears her down as a way to try to build himself up. It's also the excuse a man gives his wife or girlfriend when he gets caught cheating. That way he makes her think it was her fault he cheated on her. Whoever this Roger is, you're better off not remembering him."

"But what if he's my baby's father? What if—"

"Stop." Jack squeezed her hand, when what he wanted to do was wrap her in his arms. "Until you get your memory back, all the speculation in the world is useless. I'm sorry. I shouldn't have said anything. But damn him, Lisa, he was wrong."

She eyed Jack warily. "What do you mean?"

"When he said you weren't any good at sex. That's what you meant, wasn't it?"

Unable to look at him, she nodded.

"Look at me."

When she wouldn't, or couldn't, he carried their joined hands to her chin and nudged her face up until she met his gaze.

"I know you," he said softly. "You're the warmest, most generous woman I've ever met. There's no way he was right. If I knew for certain you weren't married, or involved with someone, I'd prove it to you.''

His words went all through Lisa, warming her blood and making her pulse race. She pressed her free hand to her chest to hold her heart in place. In his eyes she saw desire. For her.

...married, or involved...

Was she? She didn't feel as though she was, but she didn't *know*. And suddenly, here in the night, in the close confines of the vehicle, with Jack staring at her as though he could gobble her up in two big bites, she wanted desperately to know.

Oh, dear. ''I...think I better go in now.''

He held on to her hand a moment longer, then gave it another gentle squeeze. ''Stay put. I'll help you out.''

She would have objected—the last thing either of them needed was for him to put his hands on her again—but he was right. It was a long step down out of the rig, and her bulk made her less than agile.

When he got out and started around the front of the vehicle, he left the engine running and the lights on. That told her he didn't intend to go inside with her.

That was good. It was the smartest thing for both of them just then. And it was incredible how disappointed it made her feel.

The next morning Jack was in the barn doctoring a horse that hadn't seen the barbed-wire fence buried beneath the snow and had gotten cut up.

The horse didn't really need doctoring; the cuts weren't serious and would heal fine on their own. But Jack needed something to do to keep himself from going up to the house and checking on Lisa. He just wanted to look at her, to make sure she was all right, to see her smile.

But after last night...

No, he needed to stay away for a while, give her a little space. She probably wasn't in any hurry to be around him. She'd meant to thank him, and he'd turned it into something else entirely. Something neither of them was ready for.

The horse stomped a foot at Jack's lack of attention.

"Sorry, fella. I'll hurry."

Trey sauntered into the barn and up to the stall. He looked the situation over and let out a low whistle. "I've seen worse, but I don't remember when."

Jack gave him a look of dismissal. "It's just a few cuts, and none of them too bad. You've seen plenty worse."

"I was talking about you, not the gelding. Who died?"

"Nobody that I know of," Jack grumbled. "I don't know what you're talking about."

"Uh-huh." Trey leaned against the stall door. "You look like the world caved in on you. Wanna talk about it?"

Jack turned back to the horse and dabbed antiseptic on another cut. "Nothing to talk about."

"Ah."

"What's that supposed to mean? Ah. Ah, what?"

"It means, big brother, that whenever a man says there's nothing to talk about, it usually indicates woman trouble."

Jack snorted.

"You got woman trouble, Jack?"

Jack refused to look at his younger brother. He knew that if he did he'd find Trey grinning like a possum. He could hear that grin in his voice. "You know damn well and good I don't have a woman. No woman, no woman trouble."

"There you have it."

"I know I'm gonna regret asking this, but there I have what?"

"The source of your trouble. No woman."

Jack snorted again. "Okay, wise guy, where's your woman?"

"I happen to be between women right now."

Jack purposely took the comment in a way he knew Trey hadn't meant and laughed. "You wish, bro."

Trey snickered. "True enough. I'd like to be between a redhead and a—"

"Spare me the details. It's too early in the morning for barroom talk."

Trey shrugged, not the least offended. "Anyway, I'll be finding myself a new woman when I get to Las Vegas after Ace and Belinda come home."

"Gonna get your heart broken by some long-legged showgirl?"

"I hope so," Trey said with feeling. "I dearly hope so. Hey, you're not still mooning over Marsha, are you?"

"Get real. That's ancient history."

Trey nodded. "Yeah, okay. That narrows it down, then. You're mooning over Lisa."

Jack ground his teeth together to keep from saying anything. No matter what he might say, Trey would twist it around and make something out of nothing. Better to just keep his mouth shut. Except that didn't stop Trey, either.

"No comment?"

Jack slathered too much ointment on another small cut. "I wouldn't dignify such an absurd remark by commenting."

"Well, then," Trey said a little too casually, "I guess that means you won't mind if I mosey on up to the house and pay her a visit."

Jack whirled on Trey so fast he startled the horse. The animal shied and stepped on Jack's foot.

The string of curses that Jack let out turned the air blue. Trey laughed till he nearly split a gut. Jack finished swearing long before Trey finished laughing.

"It wasn't that funny," Jack muttered, turning back to soothe the horse.

When he could talk again, Trey let out a gusty sigh. "Oh, yeah, it was."

"I don't recall you thinking it was too damn funny when you got kicked in the shin last month."

Trey chuckled. "I wasn't laughing at the fool horse stepping on you. I was laughing at the look on your face when I said I was gonna go up to the house and see Lisa. Guess that told me what I want to know."

Jack shot him a dirty look. "She's got enough trouble on her hands without having to fight off some jerk who thinks he's the local Don Juan."

"Well, then, you oughtta stay away from her."

"You're so damn funny, aren't you? I'm telling *you* to stay away from her."

"I rest my case," Trey said. "You want her for yourself. You're mooning over her."

"You don't know what you're talking about. She doesn't need *any* man stirring up things for her just now."

"Yeah," Trey said, turning serious. "She's in a

bad spot, all right, with her memory gone and a baby on the way. Is she married? Is that what's got you tied up in knots?''

Jack worked his way down a series of shallow cuts on the horse's right foreleg and said nothing.

"Damn," Trey said. "So that's it."

"No," Jack said tersely. "That's not it. Exactly."

"Not it exactly? What does that mean?"

Jack leaned his head on the horse's neck. "Jeez, you're gonna worry this to death, aren't you?"

"Hey, there's only the two of us left in this family who are still single. I'm just looking out for you, bro. It's not like you to fall for a married woman."

"First of all," Jack said, eyes narrowed, "I haven't fallen for her. Second, it's not that she's married, it's that she doesn't *know* if she's married."

Trey let out a long whistle. "Wow. That's rough, man. Hell of a thing to forget."

"She can't help it."

"I know. What are you gonna do?"

"Nothing." Jack turned back to the horse. "Not a damn thing."

As noon approached, the temperature shot upward and the snow began to melt rapidly. Lisa was amazed that every time she looked out a window there was less and less of the white stuff. There was still a lot of it; there'd been so much to begin with. They wouldn't see bare ground anytime soon, but the piles and drifts were visibly shrinking. The sight should have boosted her spirits, but it didn't.

She sat staring at the television. There was a talk show on, and she hoped it would take her mind off herself for a while, but no luck there, either.

She had neither seen nor heard from Jack since last night. She couldn't decide if she should be unhappy or relieved. Unhappy because she wanted to see him, relieved because she needed this time to think clearly.

Clearly. That was a laugh. Everything in her head was muddled and fuzzy, or sharp and confusing.

She was pregnant, so that meant there was a man somewhere in her life. At least there had been. But the picture she was getting of him did nothing to reassure her that everything would be fine once her memory fully returned.

Who was this Roger who thought she was no good at sex?

Jack had been right about that. Lisa had called it "man-woman stuff." But what she knew—she couldn't truthfully call it a memory, because she couldn't remember a Roger—was that this Roger person had told her—no, convinced her, for she believed it—that she was no good at sex.

A man wouldn't make a statement like that unless he'd had sex with her, would he? He hadn't said, "I hear..." He'd said, "You are..."

Did that mean Roger was the father of her baby? Was he the man she was angry with? She had told Jack that her baby might never know its father if the jerk didn't back off.

Then there was the money she'd brought with her. And her medical records.

Everything pointed to the assumption that she and the baby's father had had a falling-out, and that she hadn't planned to return to Denver anytime soon.

Oh, Lord, she wished she could just remember!

Maybe, if she could remember her past, remember herself, she would know what to do with these mixed feelings she had for Jack. Wary one minute, yearning the next. And sometimes, like last night when her lips had brushed his, downright turned on.

She felt like a yo-yo, some giant unseen hand yanking her string.

How long could she go on like this? What if her memory didn't return for months, or years, or never?

She needed a plan. A plan that would allow her to stand on her own. Obviously she needed to know if she was married. She supposed she could go to Denver and check the courthouse records.

Of course if she found nothing, that would only mean she hadn't gotten married in that county. She could have gotten married anywhere.

She could hire a detective to find out about her life, but was that the best use of her money when she would have a baby to care for, medical bills, living expenses? Heavens, she would go broke in no time.

She would need a job and a place to live. She couldn't live off the Wilders, even if Belinda really was her best friend. But the job would have to wait. When she'd looked over her medical records, she'd learned that the baby was due sooner than she'd thought. When she had remembered that she was seven months pregnant, she must have been remembering how far along she'd been at her last checkup. She was now, as of yesterday, eight months along. No one was going to hire her that close to her due date, only to have her take off for six weeks in a scant month. Assuming she would be able to work that long.

No, the job would have to wait. She could have the baby in Hope Springs. Maybe there was a small house for rent there. The thought of going somewhere else, where she wouldn't know a single person, left her cold.

"Lisa?"

At the sound of Jack's voice she gave a start.

"Sorry. I didn't mean to scare you. I knocked and called out. Guess you didn't hear me."

She pushed herself up from the couch. "I guess I didn't. I was…watching television." She felt her cheeks sting at the small lie. She'd been *staring* at the television, but she had no idea what was on.

Jack stuffed his hands in his pockets and took a step back toward the kitchen. "I was just going to help myself to something for lunch."

Lisa insisted on fixing something for him. "How much time do you have before you need to get back to work?"

"Some. Why?"

He was a hardworking man. He needed something more substantial than a sandwich or two, and he had to be getting tired of soup from a can. "I could fry a chicken."

His grin came slow and wide. "I'll take the time."

To her surprise and pleasure, he stayed in the kitchen with her while she cooked. He sat at the kitchen table and stretched his legs out, and they talked a little about the warmer weather.

"I found a ham in the freezer," she told him. "I thought I'd bake that this afternoon for tonight's supper."

"Sounds good."

"Will you tell the others?"

He chuckled. "If you're going to make me share with them, I guess I don't have a choice."

"Don't worry, there'll be plenty for everyone."

They fell silent while she worked, but it was such an easy silence that she found herself humming. When she realized she was humming the Anne Murray tune they had danced to at the section house, she stopped and cast Jack a surreptitious look.

He was watching her, his eyes dark and steady.

She looked away quickly and checked the same piece of chicken she'd just checked.

By the time the meal was done and on the table, the silence didn't feel as comfortable as it had. Probably because Lisa had suddenly thought to wonder if she had combed her hair in the past few hours. Or maybe she had flour on her face. Something was making Jack stare at her, and she was becoming more self-conscious by the minute.

For something to say, she asked him if there was a local newspaper for the area.

"A small weekly." He reached for another piece of chicken. "The *Wyatt County Gazette*. Should be one in the mail later today. I'll bring it when I come for supper."

"Thank you. I want to look for a place to live."

He paused with a drumstick halfway to his mouth. "You're going to stay in Wyoming?"

"Yes. I've been thinking about it all day," she added in a rush. "I think I must have planned to stay and have the baby here. Why else would I have brought all that cash and my medical records? I'll need a job after the baby comes, of course, but that shouldn't be—"

"Lisa, it's all right."

She stopped and took a slow breath. She'd been talking so fast it was a wonder he'd even understood her.

"You don't have to justify anything to anybody. If you want to stay here and have your baby, nobody's going to say you can't. But there's no hurry to find a job or a place to live. You know you've got a place to stay right here for as long as you want."

Oh, dear. Sir Jack was going to get all knightly on her. She loved it when he did that. It was so sweet and made her feel cared for. She had no intention of arguing with him about it, either. "I'm not going to hurry," she assured him. "I just wanted to look at the paper and get an idea of what might be available."

Jack didn't like this talk of Lisa's about finding a place to live. He was surprised at how strongly he was against it. Dammit, she had a place to live—right there on the Flying Ace.

Well, okay, so she might not want to live off Belinda forever, especially since she had no memory of her or their friendship.

And okay, so the section house would only be available to her until he hired a new section foreman in a couple of months.

That doesn't leave much, pard, came a smart-mouthed voice from inside his head.

Right. It didn't leave her much of an alternative. But he intended to talk her into staying right where she was until after the baby was born and she had recovered from childbirth. She would have help here, from Belinda and Donna.

But he'd promised her the newspaper, so he would take it to her. Reluctantly, but he would take it.

He took it to her that night when he went up to the house for supper. When she set it aside until after the meal, he was relieved. Maybe that meant she wasn't as eager to find a place as he'd feared.

Her ham with all the trimmings was a big hit with everyone. She'd even gone to the trouble of baking a pecan pie for dessert.

"I guess there are some things a woman just never forgets," Trey said with a devilish grin.

Lisa smiled sweetly. "What would that be?"

The twinkle in Trey's eyes sparkled. "Cooking."

Her smile widened. "Was that by any chance a chauvinistic remark?"

"Well…"

Stoney was fighting a smile and swinging his gaze between Trey and Lisa.

"Since Belinda isn't here," Jack offered lazily, "I'll say it for her. Shut up, Number Three."

Stoney and Trey laughed.

Lisa chuckled. "I take it Trey was trying to see if I'd get fired up over a comment like that. Would Belinda?"

"She wouldn't have just boxed his ears," Stoney offered. "She would have sliced them off and served them at the next meal."

Trey laughed and shuddered. "That's a little too close to the truth for comfort."

"Hmm." Lisa smiled. "I can't wait to remember her. I think I must really like that woman."

"Pardon me for saying so," Trey told her, "but for best friends, you and Belinda seem as different as night and day."

"How do you mean?" Lisa asked.

"Opposites," Jack offered.

"No kidding," Trey said. "The fox is all starch and vinegar, while you're more…"

"Go on," Lisa encouraged.

Jack watched with interest as the gleam in Lisa's eyes sharpened. He'd seen her upset, devastated, thoughtful, happy. He'd seen anger in her eyes when she spoke about the baby's father the other day without realizing what she'd been saying. But he'd never seen quite this look of...calculation? Was that it? Or was it more a promise of retribution the minute Trey stepped into the hole he'd dug for himself?

"I, uh, think I'll quit while I'm ahead." Trey took a big bite of ham to occupy his mouth so he wouldn't have to say anything else.

"You're a wise man," Lisa said with a nod.

"Maybe they're not so different, after all," Trey muttered.

"I heard that," Lisa said.

When the other men left for the night, Jack stayed behind to help Lisa clean up the kitchen.

"I can do this," she protested. "You've been working all day. Go sit down and put your feet up."

Grinning, Jack carried another load of dirty dishes to the counter. "Boy, you *are* different from Belinda."

"She would let you help?"

"Hell, no. If Ace didn't pay a housekeeper to do all this, Belinda would be the one walking out and putting her feet up while the men did the cleaning."

"I wish I could remember her," she said wistfully.

Jack put the dishes down and cupped a hand on her shoulder. "You will. You're starting to remember a little more every day."

"I know, but it's coming so slowly that it's frustrating.'' She shook her head. ''To think that I know someone that strong when I feel like such a wimp.''

''Wimp?'' Jack turned her around until she faced him. ''How can you say that? You're just about the strongest woman I've ever known.''

''Me?'' she said, clearly astounded.

''Yes, you. You were obviously in some sort of bad situation in Denver, whatever it was, so you decided to do something about it. You called on a friend for a place to stay, and you came up here regardless of the fact that you were pregnant and alone. Do you have any idea how much guts it takes to do something like that? Leave everything familiar to you, turn your entire life upside down at a time when a woman is at her most vulnerable?''

Lisa swallowed. ''None of that sounds particularly smart or strong to me. It sounds weak. It sounds like I couldn't handle my life, so I simply ran away.''

''Sometimes running away *is* the smart thing to do. Don't judge yourself that way until you know why you left Denver. You're not a wimp, Lisa. Look at the way you've handled yourself since you got here.''

''Oh, yeah. I wrecked my car and gave myself a concussion,'' she said with disgust. ''That was real smart and brave of me.''

''Anybody ever tell you you need to work on your self-image? You're deliberately putting yourself down. I'm talking about coming to after that accident and having no memory of anything. You were stranded with a strange man in what could easily have become a life-threatening situation, and you never batted an eye. I'm with Trey on that. If it was me, I'd end up in a padded cell. But not you. You're handling it. *Admirable* isn't a word I use often, but that's what you are."

Lisa was, quite simply, overwhelmed. "Jack—"

"When I said you and Belinda were opposites, I only meant that she's tough-as-nails, in-your-face aggressive, while you're softer, gentler. The two of you complement each other."

"Jack...I don't know what to say."

He stepped back and dropped his hands from her shoulders. "Say, 'Yes, Jack, you're absolutely right. I'm a brave and wonderful person.'"

She blushed. "You know I can't say words like that." She smiled and turned back to the sink. "But you're entitled to your opinion."

They worked together easily, as if they'd been doing it for years, despite Lisa's nerves being on edge over the things Jack had said about her.

He was wrong. She wasn't a brave person, a smart person. If she were either, she surely wouldn't be having a baby alone in Wyoming among strangers.

"I forgot to tell you," Jack said. "There was a message on my answering machine this evening from Curly."

"The auto mechanic?"

"That's right. He has to order a part for your car, so it'll be at least a week before it's ready. If you need to go anywhere before then, you can use one of the ranch rigs."

"Thank you."

"You're welcome." What Jack didn't tell her was that he had instructed Curly to check her car over from front to back, inside and out, and fix every single thing that needed fixing.

"Pretend," Jack had told him, "that your grandmother is going to drive that car from here to Florida with your kids in the back seat.''

He'd told Curly to bill him for anything above the original estimate and not to mention any of this to Lisa.

Jack and Lisa finished cleaning up the kitchen together, then Lisa took the newspaper he had brought her and settled at the kitchen table to check the classifieds.

"I'm afraid you're not going to find much there,'' Jack warned.

"Looks like you're right. Two apartments are all that's listed under rental property. Oh, look at that,'' she cried.

"What?'' Jack leaned over her shoulder to see what had her so excited.

"This car, see? This one.''

It was a twenty-some-year-old Pontiac Trans Am, pictured in the middle of a half-page ad for a dealership up in Pinedale. "What about it?''

"It looks just like the first car I ever owned. God, I loved that car. I never should have sold it.''

Jack's pulse sped up. She was remembering again and didn't even realize it. Maybe if he didn't point that out to her, she might remember more. He rounded the table as casually as he could and slipped into the chair across from her. "Why did you sell it?''

She tilted her head and stared over his shoulder at the wall. "I...I don't know. Oh, damn, it's happened again. I saw that picture and remembered my car, then it's like a door slammed in my head and cut off all the other memories.'' She pounded a fist on the table. "I feel like if I just think hard enough or long enough, it'll come to me.''

Jack reached across the table and covered her fist with his hand. "But you're remembering more every day. That's the important thing."

She let out a long breath, then gave him a look. "All right, Pollyanna."

Jack burst out laughing. "No one's ever called me that before."

During the next two days Lisa realized that Jack was coming to the house every couple of hours on one pretext or another. He never stayed long, except after dinner. And now, today, he lingered after lunch.

She couldn't blame him for wanting to stay in the house today. Those warmer temperatures of the past two days were long gone, and the wind was bitterly cold. She was snug in the house, and it felt good to have Jack there.

They were sitting at the kitchen table—their favorite spot, it seemed—drinking coffee. As usual, Jack had left his boots in the mudroom.

"When do you expect Belinda and her husband to get back?" she asked. "You never said exactly."

"I'm not sure exactly," he replied. "They left the phone number of the resort where they're staying. I've tried to call a couple of times to let Belinda know what's happened, but—"

"Oh, no," Lisa protested. "Don't intrude on their vacation because of me."

"Lisa, you're her best friend. She would want to know. In fact, I can guarantee that if she gets home and *then* finds out, she'll have both our hides for not letting her know sooner. If it was your friend, wouldn't you want to know?"

"Well, when you put it that way... I just hate the

thought of disturbing them when they're having a good time. There's nothing they can do for me that they aren't already doing.''

"They're not doing anything for you, because they don't know what's happened to you."

"But they are," she objected. "More than they think, too. They believe I'm out at that cute little house near the hills. Instead, I've invaded their home."

"You haven't invaded anything," Jack countered. ''I brought you here, and I own part of this house, so don't worry about it. Anyway, I wasn't able to reach them, so I just left a message asking them to call. I had to tell them it wasn't urgent so they wouldn't think something had happened to one of the boys."

At the sound of the front doorbell he halted and frowned. "What the hell? Nobody comes to the front door around here." He pushed himself up and headed for the living room.

Lisa followed more slowly and arrived in time to see him open the front door.

A man stood on the porch. He was an attractive man, very sleek and polished, with a hint of arrogance in the way he held his head. His knee-length leather coat, salon-styled hair and Italian shoes all shouted money.

As Jack pushed open the glass storm door, the stranger looked past him to Lisa. A smile lit his face, but not, she noticed, his hard brown eyes. "Lisa! Darling, I've been so worried about you!"

At the sound of his voice something inside Lisa turned cold, then heat flushed through her. "I'm sorry," she managed. "Do I know you?"

"Come on, sweetheart." His smile turned sarcastic.

"You know you're no good at humor." He tugged off his leather gloves and carefully put them in the pockets of his coat. "I'll help you get your things together. I've come to take you home."

Beside her, Lisa felt Jack practically vibrate with a sudden sharp tension that mirrored what was happening in her. She felt that same tension from the top of her head to the soles of her feet. "Who are you?"

He started to step through the doorway, but Jack braced an arm against the jamb and blocked him. "The lady asked you a question."

"What's going on here?" the man demanded. "Stop kidding around, Lisa, and let's go."

Lisa shook her head and backed away. "I don't know you."

"I don't know what kind of game you're playing," he said tersely, "but I'm tired of it."

"I'm not playing a game." Lisa tried to calm herself, but so many different emotions assailed her that she didn't know what she felt. But something about this man made her leery. She put a hand to the bruise on her forehead. "I was in an accident. I'm afraid I'm having a little trouble with my memory."

Roger stared at her, stunned. He realized she was telling the truth. She had no idea who he was. Lisa was, if anything, entirely too honest. She didn't know how to lie.

"Amnesia?" he asked, incredulous.

"I'm afraid so," she answered.

Roger glanced at the man blocking his way and eased back. The man looked just uncouth and primitive enough to resort to physical violence at the drop of a hat.

Amnesia. Who would have thought? It was perfect.

Roger nearly chuckled with glee, but instead, put on a sober demeanor. "Honey, I'm so sorry!" he cried. "How terrible. We'll get you to the best doctors money can buy the minute we get home."

The man blocking the door practically growled.

Roger hadn't gotten to be one of the top attorneys in Denver without learning how to read people. This man was furious.

If Roger's detective had done his homework correctly, and if this was the man Lisa had been with in town the other day, then he would be Jack Wilder, one of the owners of this ranch.

What the hell was Lisa doing here? Had she known this man long? How dare she run straight to Wilder's arms when she belonged to *him*.

"The lady asked who you are," Wilder snarled. "We're still waiting for an answer."

"My pardon," Roger offered easily. "I'm Roger Hampton. I'm Lisa's husband."

Chapter Eight

"**No!**" Lisa stepped back and shook her head, panic threatening to overwhelm her. She could not possibly be married to this condescending, arrogant…

No. It couldn't be true. She remembered how, when she'd come to in her car and Jack had carried her into the house and she'd discovered she was pregnant, she'd instinctively known that, yes, the pregnancy felt right. Felt familiar.

She had no such feeling of rightness at this man's bald claim that he was her husband.

But you know a man named Roger.

Yes. A man named Roger had told her she was no good in bed. Would a husband say such a thing to a wife?

You have the same last name.

Standing there staring at him, wanting only for him to disappear, a flash of memory assailed her, chilling her to the bone and making her stomach turn. A memory of waking up in bed with this man. It was just a flash, and she could feel no emotion with it, neither hers nor his, but for a second it was there.

Then another flash, this one only a feeling rather than a memory—a feeling of inadequacy, inferiority. A feeling of being less than a woman. A feeling of being used and made a fool of.

This man, this Roger Hampton, was obviously *something* to her, but her husband? She prayed not!

"I'm sorry." She couldn't seem to catch her breath. "I don't know you."

"Lisa, honey, you said you've been in an accident. I'll get you to a doctor and everything will be all right, you'll see."

"I've been to a doctor." She was becoming really irritated with the way he spoke to her, as though she were an imbecile. "Going to a doctor isn't going to bring back my memory. How did you find me?"

He looked startled at her question. "What? It, well, it wasn't a question of *finding* you. I knew where you were."

Suspicion sharpened her voice. "How?"

"Why, naturally you told me you were coming here."

No, Lisa thought. She didn't think so. She had gathered her medical records and several thousand dollars in cash and then told him where she was going? That didn't make sense. But then, none of this made sense, so he could be telling the truth.

God, she was confused!

"Come on, honey, let's get your things and go home."

The thought of leaving with this man made her decidedly uneasy.

Well, of course. He was a stranger; she didn't remember him.

But what if he *was* her husband? Shouldn't she go with him?

"Honey?"

"No." She couldn't do it. "If you're who you say you are, then I'm sorry, but I can't go with you."

Anger flashed in his eyes. "Don't be difficult." He shoved past Jack and reached for her arm.

In a blink Jack was on him. He grabbed Roger by the shoulder and spun him around. "You lay a hand on her, and I'll have to mess up that pretty face of yours."

"Are you threatening me?"

"You better believe it."

Roger seethed. "Since she doesn't remember me, allow me to explain," he said through clenched teeth. "I am an attorney. I will sue you for all your worth, which probably isn't much."

"Now let *me* explain," Jack said, his voice low and cold. "You're a trespasser in my home, presenting a physical threat to a woman under my protection. And if you still don't understand, consider this. Dead men can't sue anybody."

Roger sucked in a sharp breath and stuck out his chest. "You're making a mistake."

"Please," Lisa said. God, she didn't want anyone hurt because of her. "Please just go, Mr. Hampton. Roger. If you're really my husband, you'll still be my husband after I've had some time to think this through."

"Why, of course I will." Roger's stance eased as

he turned back to Lisa. Between one breath and the next, the lines of anger on his face turned to contrition. "I apologize. I understand that with your memory loss, you need a little time to get used to the idea. But wouldn't it be better if I stayed here with you so you could learn to be comfortable around me?"

She shook her head. "No. There's a motel in town, isn't there, Jack?"

"Yes."

"You could stay there," she told Roger, "until I've decided what I'm going to do."

With obvious reluctance, Roger agreed. "I'll be back tomorrow."

"No," she said again. "I'm going to need a few days." He opened his mouth to object, but she rushed on. "I appreciate your patience. I'm sure you'll understand that I would be foolish to simply take your word for everything when you're a stranger to me."

"But, darling, unless you get your memory back, I'll still be a stranger to you in a few days. Why wait?"

Lisa backed away from him. "Because that's the way I want it." She kept her tone reasonable when what she wanted to do was scream at him to get away from her and not come back. She didn't want to remember him. Didn't want to know she was married to him. *God, please, don't let me be married to him.*

"Very well," he finally said. "I'll be back day after tomorrow."

"You'll stay away," Jack said, "until she calls you at the motel and asks you to come back."

Lisa wrapped her arms around herself and watched the man named Roger Hampton get in his shiny black BMW and drive away.

Jack closed the door and turned toward her. "Are you all right?" She didn't look all right to him. Her face was ashen and she was shaking so badly it was a wonder she was still standing.

"I...I don't want to remember him," she blurted.

Some of the tension that had tied his stomach in knots the minute the man had introduced himself eased. She didn't want to remember Roger Hampton.

But the question had to be asked. "Could he be telling the truth?"

Lisa looked at Jack with such devastation on her face that it hurt to see it. "Why would he lie? He hadn't known about my amnesia. He wouldn't have known that I couldn't deny anything he said. We even have the same last name. Oh, God, what am I going to do, Jack? What am I going to do?"

There was a need in Jack every bit as big as the need he saw and sensed in Lisa. A need so huge he couldn't deny it one second longer. Right or wrong, he couldn't stop himself and didn't even try. He slipped his arms around her and held her close.

"I don't know," he told her truthfully. "But I know what you're not going to do. You're not going to do anything, and I mean *anything*, that you're uncomfortable with. You hear me?"

With her face buried against his shoulder, she murmured what he hoped was a yes.

"If that man makes you uncomfortable, you don't have to have anything to do with him."

Jack's reassurance was balm to Lisa's soul. As always, when she needed him, he was there in exactly the way she needed him to be. Always strong. Always gentle.

Oh, God, why couldn't she have a husband like him?

"Do you hear me?"

"I hear you."

But it wasn't right, holding him, leaning on him, letting him take care of her. She would be a mother soon. How was she to take care of a child and give it a good life if she couldn't straighten out her own life?

Slowly she pulled away and gazed into his eyes. "Thank you," she whispered.

His hands trailed across her back to her arms. "For what?"

"For not reminding me that a wife belongs with her husband. I believe that, you know. I believe it strongly. That when two people marry, they should stand beside each other."

"So do I," he said, "to a point. But sometimes, Lisa, things don't work out the way we plan."

She gave a wry chuckle and pulled completely free of his touch. "Don't I know it." She felt cold without his touch. "I doubt that when I came to Wyoming I planned to lose my memory. I just wish I knew what I *had* planned," she added with a mixture of fear and frustration.

"It'll come," Jack told her gently. "Just give it time. You're remembering more every day."

"Bits and pieces. Just enough to make me crazy."

"It's only been a few days," he reminded her.

"I know, I know. And I was doing all right until he showed up."

"You don't have to go with him."

"I don't plan to." And with the words, her decision was made. "I shouldn't say this, because I may have to eat my words, but I don't like that man. If I find out I'm married to him, I'm not going to like myself very much, either.''

Jack tried to fight the fierce satisfaction that welled up inside him at her statement. It shouldn't matter to him how she felt about the man who claimed to be her husband. She had already remembered the name Roger in association with comments so personal only a husband or lover could have made them. The man probably was her husband.

The thought ate a hole in his gut. Which was asinine. He'd known from the moment he'd met her that she surely had a husband. Now the man had shown up. End of question.

But dammit, did it have to be *that* man? Jack didn't blame Lisa in the least for saying she didn't like Roger Hampton. There was something too...slick about him for Jack's taste. Too cold and calculating.

It's not your taste that matters, pard.

''I'll have to alter my plans,'' Lisa said. ''I can't stay here any longer and cause you trouble.''

He didn't like the sound of that, no sir, he did not. ''You're staying right here,'' Jack said emphatically. Until she got her memory back, she was too vulnerable to that smooth-talking snake Hampton. Even if the man was her husband, he should be willing to back off rather than force his will on her.

''Ace and Belinda will be home in a few days,'' he added. ''Belinda will want you here. I'm going to go try calling her again. She can tell you whether or not you've got a husband.''

Lisa watched Jack head for the wall phone in the kitchen. Calling Belinda was the logical thing to do. But what if he reached Belinda this time? Lisa wasn't sure she wanted to know for certain that she was married to Roger Hampton. *Don't let it be true. Don't let it be true.*

She got a reprieve from having her fears confirmed. There was no answer in Belinda and Ace's hotel room. But this time when Jack left a message, he stated that it was an emergency.

"The boys are fine, it's nothing like that," he told the voice mail in their room. "It's about Lisa. She needs some information and it's urgent. If you can't reach her at the main house, try me at my number. Day or night."

After he replaced the phone in the cradle, he and Lisa stared at each other a long moment, neither saying a word.

The next two days were the most miserable Lisa had ever experienced—at least in her memory, such as it was. But if she'd ever been this confused and unhappy before, she was glad she couldn't remember it.

Oh, she knew what her problem was, just as she knew there was no solution.

Her problem was her growing feelings for Jack. At every turn, he'd been there for her, supporting her— sometimes literally, she thought, remembering the times he'd carried her in his arms—boosting her spirits, making her smile and laugh. She could so easily fall in love with him.

But to what point? There was no future for her with him. First because she was most likely married. Yet even if she wasn't married, she was having another man's baby. What man would want a woman under such circumstances?

Then there was this feeling deep inside that told her she didn't have what it took to make a man happy. That she shouldn't trust her heart to a man because he would only break it. She had enough to worry about with the baby coming and a life to build and no memory of who she was or what she was capable of. She didn't need the added worry of a man in her life.

If that man turned out to be Roger Hampton, she was ashamed to admit that she could very easily put him out of her mind.

But Jack...

What would happen to her marriage if she couldn't put Jack out of her mind, out of her heart?

"Oh, God, why is this happening to me?"

Jack wasn't in any better emotional shape than Lisa. He had to force himself to stay away from her when all he wanted to do was scoop her up in his arms and claim her for himself, Roger Hampton or any other husband be damned.

Yet the feeling, the wanting to simply be with her, to hold her, touch her...*taste* her, was so out of character that Jack almost didn't recognize himself. He'd wanted other women—and had had them. But he'd never wanted like this. He didn't know what the matter was with him. If he didn't know better, he might think he was falling in love with her.

But, of course, he did know better. He didn't know the first thing about loving a woman. He honestly believed he was incapable of such a tender emotion. And if ever a woman deserved tender emotion, deserved to be loved and happy, it was Lisa. He wasn't the man for her.

Neither, in his opinion, was Roger Hampton. If Jack had to watch her walk away on that man's arm, it might just kill him.

So he stayed away from her as much as he could. No more trips to the house in the middle of the morning to see how she was doing. No more flimsy excuses to stop by in the afternoons or hang around after supper at night. He went up for lunch, but they barely spoke, and he left quickly. Supper was more of the same, but at least then Trey and Stoney were there to take up the slack in the conversation.

On top of it all, mixed in with it, was his growing frustration and anger that Belinda hadn't called back. Damn her, what were she and Ace doing that they couldn't take the time to return a phone call?

By the afternoon of the second day after Hampton's visit, Jack realized he wasn't doing anybody any favors by staying away from Lisa. He was deliberately denying himself the pleasure of her company, when she would be gone soon. What kind of idiot did that make him?

And he was essentially condemning her to solitary confinement in the house. She was stuck there with no way to go anywhere.

"Wanna go for a drive?"

At first Lisa scarcely paid any attention to Jack's question. She was so glad to see him without the excuse of a meal between them, and without the other men to act as buffers, that her heart was racing and her blood was rushing in her ears.

Then she realized what he'd asked. "A drive?" Caution crept up her spine. He had all but ignored her for most of two days—since the afternoon Roger

Hampton had shown up. Jack had deliberately backed away from her, and she had more or less encouraged him to do so.

Now he stood before her asking if she wanted to go for a drive as if there had never been any distance between them.

"Why?" she asked.

He took a deep breath, then let it out. Sadness filled his eyes. "Because you have to be tired of being cooped up in the house all the time."

"Maybe I am," she replied. "But Jack, it's not your job to entertain me. You must have work that needs doing."

"Is that a no?"

"No," she said in frustration. "I just want it clear that I don't expect favors from you."

He cocked his head and narrowed his eyes. "Why not? Not that taking you for a tour of the ranch is any kind of favor. Call it a gesture of friendship."

It was only then, when she wanted to shoot back with the fact that favors were always called in and had to be repaid, that she realized he had hurt her feelings by staying away from her. It was the hurt that wanted to fire back at him, when what she really wanted to do was step out into the sunshine with him and go for that drive.

Where had she learned that accepting favors was a costly mistake? Had Roger Hampton taught her that?

If he had, she'd be damned before she let him—husband or not—cause her to deny herself something as simple as a drive through the snowy countryside. Nor was she going to let her own hurt feelings keep her from accepting Jack's invitation, even if Jack himself had contributed to that hurt.

She was going for herself. It wasn't healthy, for her or the baby, to shut herself up in the house this way. She needed a little fresh air and sunshine, and a little company other than her own.

She was not going just for the chance to be with Jack.

Oh, Lisa, when did you start lying to yourself?

She conveniently ignored that voice in her head. "A tour of the ranch?" she asked. "You mean I didn't see most of it the day you brought me here?"

Jack smiled. "Not hardly. Come on, let's find you a pair of Belinda's boots in case you want to get out of the rig somewhere to stretch your legs."

Jack's *not hardly* had been an understatement. They started by driving the two miles to the mailbox to get the day's mail. From there, as she recalled from the day they'd gone to town, it was another thirteen miles east to the nearest pavement. But this time, instead of heading east, Jack turned north for five miles to another east-west gravel road that ran along the north side of the Flying Ace.

The sky was so clear and bright that it almost hurt to look at it. But for the mountains looming in the west, the land looked flat, but now and then Lisa caught a glimpse of dips and rises, which told her the flatness was deceptive. A line of winter-bare trees marked the occasional creek or stream. Here and there she spotted glossy black cattle, or sometimes rich russet, grouped together around what was left of the hay bales Jack, Trey and Stoney had hauled to them after the blizzard.

"The farming operations are along the north side," Jack told her. "The first field here is alfalfa."

Lisa bit back a smile. If it was alfalfa, it was still buried. "Looks like snow to me."

"Smart aleck."

"Did you have to plow this road? It looks like it goes on forever."

"It goes far enough—all the way to the mountains. Trey plowed a stretch of it. So did Stan Kovic, the neighbor west of here. But it's a county road, so the county took care of clearing it from here to the highway. Stoney plowed the rest of the ranch roads."

In a few minutes they neared a house with a barn and several other outbuildings.

"Is that part of the ranch?" Lisa asked.

"Uh-huh. That's Trey's house. He's our farmer. Takes care of the crops."

After they passed the house, Jack pointed out another field. "Winter wheat."

It, too, was still covered in several inches of snow. "Gee, it looks just like alfalfa to me."

Jack chuckled.

As they neared the foothills, Jack turned back south and crossed a cattle guard. "We're back on Flying Ace land now."

A house stood near the turnoff, one of the Flying Ace's two section houses, complete with barn, corrals and several sheds. Five miles farther along the road sat the other section house, the one where Jack and Lisa had taken shelter during the blizzard. The one where she'd put her car in the ditch.

"It seems strange," she said, "seeing something familiar."

"It's all a matter of perspective," Jack said lazily. "To me it seems odd to see something unfamiliar."

"Are you teasing me about my sieve of a brain?"

"It's not your brain that's got holes in it, it's just your memory. Anyway, you're tough. I figure you can take a little teasing."

Lisa grinned to herself. She couldn't be sure, but it felt as though she hadn't been playfully teased much in recent years, if ever. She liked it.

They were about halfway between the site of her accident and ranch headquarters when Lisa spotted another side road taking off to the south. "I don't remember seeing that the last time we came this way."

"You wouldn't have. It wasn't plowed yet."

"Where does it go?"

"To the cemetery."

Lisa blinked. "You have your own cemetery?"

"You bet. It goes back five generations. Well, three, since none of us has died yet."

"What a thing to say."

"Well, we haven't, so there are only three generations there." He thought a minute as they neared the road. "Actually there are four generations. Cathy, Ace's first wife, is buried there."

"Is it very far?"

"Just over the hill. You wanna stop?"

"Could we? I have a thing for cemeteries that dates back years and years. There's something about them that always makes me feel a connection with those who came before. Does that sound silly?"

Jack slowed and turned onto the road to the cemetery. "No," he said. "But it does sound like you just found another piece of your memory."

"Good grief." Lisa hugged herself and smiled. "It just felt so natural to say that, to think it. I might not have realized it was a new memory if you hadn't pointed it out.''

But then she was hugging herself not from pleasure, but from dismay. The more of her memory that returned, the sooner she would remember Roger Hampton. She didn't want to think about that man. It would ruin her day.

She wanted to hear Jack's voice again. The sound of it would keep her grounded in the present. ''Do you visit the cemetery often enough that you have to keep the road plowed in the winter?''

Jack took the hill slowly. ''Not the way you mean. I'll show you when we get up there.''

The plowed road led up and around one low hill, then another. These weren't the small hills she'd seen in other parts of the ranch. Here there were rocky outcroppings, sharp drops into gullies and ravines. Piñon grew here, and deciduous trees that she couldn't identify in their winter bareness.

Lisa didn't know for sure, but this area looked more suitable for goats than cattle.

Then they rounded a bend and came out on what looked to be the highest point of land until the foothills to the west, a mostly bald top swept free of snow by the wind.

The small cemetery, hosting maybe two dozen graves, was enclosed by a tall barbed-wire fence.

''You're afraid someone might try to leave?'' Lisa asked, her lips twitching.

Jack rolled his eyes. ''The fence is to keep out the cattle and horses, and hopefully the moose, elk, deer—''

''I get the picture.'' She loved the look of it, lonely and windswept, yet with a peacefulness about it. The dozen or more granite headstones, several tilted at odd angles, looked as cold as the winter sky, but that didn't put Lisa off.

Jack parked the truck and came around to help her out. He led her through the gate and into the grave-yard.

The piñons growing in two corners looked as if they'd grown there naturally, but surely someone had planted the tall pine near the gate. The only other pines were high in the mountains.

"Are your parents buried here?" she asked Jack softly.

"Yeah. Over there." He pointed and led her in that direction.

"I'm sorry they're dead, but it must be comforting to know they're here, that you can come visit them, talk to them, whenever you want."

"Where are your folks?" Jack asked her. He, too, spoke softly, as if reluctant to disturb the quiet.

"I don't know. I've never known. They disap-peared when I was three. They were presumed dead, but their bodies were never found. Oh, my God," she added, stunned. "I remember that!"

"Remember what, specifically?"

"Oh, not being three, but I remember that I've never known my parents."

Jack thought if he could keep her talking, instead of thinking, she might accidentally remember even more. "Did you live with relatives after your parents disappeared?"

"I...I lived...ah, damn!" She pressed her finger-tips to her forehead and grimaced. "I had it. Dammit, I had it. It was right there, then it was gone."

"It's okay." He took her hand from her forehead and held it in both of his. "It's okay. Don't—"

"Push it. I know, I know. But why won't it just *come?*"

"I don't know." He cupped her cheek in one palm and ached at the pain he saw in her eyes. "If I could bring your memory back for you…"

He let his words trail off, unfinished. He didn't want her to go through this agony. He wanted her to regain her memory. But if he could, he would block whatever she might remember about Roger Hampton. Whoever the man was, he had hurt her in the past. Instinct told Jack that given the chance, the man would hurt her again.

Hell, Jack thought. He'd brought her out on this drive to get both their minds off Hampton. With an effort he pulled back and took her by the arm.

"Here," he said, taking on the tone of a tour guide, "is the original owner of this land. At least, the original white man to have title."

"Conner?" Lisa read on the headstone.

"That's right, Jeremiah Conner, for whom the phrase 'bet the farm' must have been invented, because he did. Literally. He lost the deed to this land in a poker game with that fellow over there." He pointed to another grave ten feet away.

"The English baron?"

"Uh-huh. John Wilder. The first Wilder in Wyoming."

"But obviously not the last," Lisa noted.

"Not by a long shot. Next to him is his wife, Elizabeth Comstock Wilder of the New England Comstocks, or so the story goes."

He went on to show her the graves of the rest of

his ancestors: John and Elizabeth's only son, Earl, and Earl's wife Suzannah, then Jack's father and stepmother, King and Betty Wilder, and Ace's first wife, Cathy.

"Who's buried over there?" Lisa asked, fascinated by the history, the continuity of family, one generation into the next, into the next and into the next.

"Some of the men who've worked here over the years, who died here and had no place else to go."

One grave, however, stood out. "Why is that one decorated while the others aren't?" Lisa asked.

"That's our mystery. That's why we plow the road up here in winter, so we can check to see if she's been here."

"She?"

"Or he." Jack shrugged. "Whoever it is who parks somewhere on the county road along the south side of the ranch and hikes anywhere from two to five miles to get up here, sometimes in the dead of night, to leave fresh flowers or pine boughs several times a year."

"You mean you don't have any idea who's doing it? Or who's buried here?"

"Nobody knows. The deceased is a stranger my dad found out here somewhere before I came to live here. The body was never identified or claimed, so it was just buried here."

"How sad, but fascinating. Do you think whoever leaves these things here knows who the man was?"

"I'd have to say yes, since, as far as we know, nobody else in this part of the state gets mysterious decorations on their graves. Once it was a bottle of scotch. Seems like an odd thing for a woman to leave, but we've tracked her a time or two, and it's either a woman or a man with pretty small feet."

"Or a boy?"

"Possibly, but I'm guessing it's an adult. Hell, it's been going on for so many years now, we might be into the second or third generation of them."

"I think it's romantic. To care that deeply about someone even after they're gone. A friend probably wouldn't go to so much trouble. It must be family." She turned and looked around at all the graves again. "It must be comforting to know that even in death you'll be surrounded by family."

Jack saw the wistful look in her eyes, heard it in her voice. She was thinking again that she had no family.

He wished...

Ah, hell. He wished Belinda would call and put an end to the mystery of Roger Hampton.

That night after supper the call from Belinda finally came. Stoney and Trey had already left the house, the kitchen was cleaned up, and Jack was in the mudroom putting on his boots so that he, too, could leave, when the phone rang.

Stooped over in the act of tugging on his left boot, Jack froze and looked up at Lisa. She stood in the middle of the kitchen, stock-still, like a deer caught in headlights. For a long moment neither moved. Somehow they knew that this was the call that would answer the question that had been eating at both of them. And somehow, both were unsure if they were ready to hear the answer.

Then the phone rang a second time and broke the

spell. With a curse Jack jerked his boot in place and grabbed for the phone.

"Belinda? It's about damn time. Yeah, she's here. Just a minute." He held the phone out to Lisa. "She wants to talk to you."

Lisa stared at the phone as if it were a snake. "I don't know what to say."

"Do you want me to—"

"No." Lisa squared her shoulders and reached for the phone. She had to start standing on her own and stop expecting Jack to take care of things for her. "No, I'll do it." She took the phone from Jack and put it to her ear. "Hello?"

"Hey, girlfriend," came a friendly female voice. "What's wrong? You didn't up and have that baby before we got home, did you?"

Lisa gripped the receiver more tightly. That voice! Something about that voice pulled at her. "No," she answered. She had to hear the woman talk. "How's Hawaii?" *Say something, say anything. Just let me hear your voice again.*

The woman on the other end of the line let out a husky laugh. "How is it? Well, I'll tell you, Lisa my friend, they don't call it paradise for nothing. But I don't imagine that was the emergency, was it? I ask again, what's wrong? You know you can't keep a secret from me. Spill it."

Oh, God. Lisa didn't know if she could go through with it. She didn't know if she could get any words out past the huge lump in her throat. Whenever she looked in a mirror, she didn't recognize herself. A man told her he was her husband, but she didn't know him. Now, hearing the voice of a woman who was supposed to be her best friend and not remembering that voice—it was too much. Just…too much. A sob tore from her throat.

Alarmed, Jack grabbed the phone from Lisa and shouted into it, "What the hell did you say to her?"

"Jack? Nothing. I didn't say anything. What's wrong? What's happened?"

Jack reached for Lisa. "We need some time here. Call back in five minutes."

"I will not," Belinda said hotly. "You talk to me, Jack Wilder. What's happened to Lisa?"

But Jack wasn't listening. He couldn't worry about Belinda when Lisa was falling apart before his eyes. He hung up the phone and wrapped his arms around her, holding her close. He didn't know what had set her off, but he wasn't about to let her go through this alone.

In a plush hotel room on the Kona Coast on the island of Hawaii, Belinda Wilder listened, dumbfounded, to the dial tone in her ear. "That son of a…"

"What happened?" Ace asked, puzzled.

"I'm going to kill him." She put the phone down and started pacing. "He's dead meat."

"Slim?" As her husband, Ace felt it was his duty to keep his wife from serving time. "You wanna think about that a bit?"

"We'll tell the kids he moved away. We won't need a funeral, because no one will ever find all the body parts."

"I assume you mean Jack."

"Of course I mean Jack!"

"What did he say?"

"He didn't say anything. He hung up on me!" she said incredulously. "Lisa started crying, then Jack took the phone before I could find out what was wrong. That sorry SOB *hung up* on me!''

Back in Wyoming, Jack felt like a sorry SOB. He wanted to *do* something, wanted to help, wanted to make Lisa's tears dry up and bring a smile to her face, and damn his hide, he didn't know what to do. All he could do was hold her, with her baby safely cradled between their bodies, and let her cry it out.

"That's it," he crooned. "You've been holding this in for a long time. Just let it out, cupcake, just let it out."

And she did. She held on to him as tightly as she could, got as close as the baby would allow, with her face buried against Jack's shoulder, and cried her heart out.

It tore Jack up inside to know she hurt so much, but he was glad she was finally letting go of it. She hadn't shed a tear since that first day, when she had admitted she had no memory.

Gradually her sobs dwindled to sniffles.

"That's it, cupcake. You'll feel better now."

Sniff. "Cupcake?" She raised her head and gave him a watery wobbly smile. "Why did you call me that?"

"I don't know." He reached for a tissue from the box on the counter and blotted her tears. "You're sweet, you're round…"

Lisa half-laughed, half-choked. "You're terrible."

"That's me." Jack wrapped his arms around her again and rocked her gently from side to side.

She sniffed and patted his shoulder. "I'm sorry I got you all wet. I'm sorry I fell apart like that."

"Don't apologize to me." He placed a kiss on the

top of her head. "If anybody's ever earned a crying jag, you have."

She looked over his shoulder and saw that he'd hung up the phone. "What must Belinda think?"

"Odds are she thinks I'm a jerk for hanging up on her."

"You hung up on your sister-in-law?"

He smoothed a hand over her cheek and waited until she met his gaze. "You were more important."

Lisa ducked her head. "I don't know what happened. I heard her voice and I didn't recognize it. She's supposed to be my best friend and I didn't recognize her voice. All of a sudden it was just...too much."

"You don't owe anybody any explanation," Jack said.

"I owe Belinda one." She stepped out of Jack's arms and pushed her hair off her face with both hands. "She must think I've lost my mind."

"She'll understand," Jack assured her.

"Not if we don't call her back."

The phone rang.

Jack grinned. "No need. That's her."

Lisa closed her eyes and took a deep breath.

"I'll explain—"

"No." Lisa opened her eyes and met his gaze. "Thank you. But I can't keep letting you handle my problems. I have to stand on my own."

Jack saw she was determined. "All right." He picked up the receiver on the third ring and handed it to Lisa.

The first thing Lisa did was apologize profusely. "I'm so sorry. I don't know how to explain what just happened, but I'm through feeling sorry for myself."

"Are you all right?" Belinda asked. "The baby?"

It struck Lisa then that Roger Hampton, who claimed to be her husband, had not asked about the baby. "We're both fine. I had an accident—"

"Were you hurt?" Belinda demanded.

Lisa smiled. Belinda generally demanded rather than asked.

I know that! she thought, thrilled. *I know Belinda demands, instead of asks.*

"Lisa! Dammit, girl, answer me."

"I'm sorry. Except for a bump on my forehead, I'm fine. But...oh, hell, I have amnesia."

There was a short pause before Belinda spoke. "Explain."

Lisa's lips twitched. "Amnesia, the loss of memory."

"Very funny. You haven't forgotten that little tongue-in-cheek habit of yours. What *have* you forgotten?"

"Everything. Everything about myself, my life. I had to look on my driver's license to find out what my name is."

This time the pause was longer. "You're pulling my leg, right?"

"I'm afraid not. I don't...I don't recognize your voice, yet Jack says you're my best friend."

"Maybe I won't kill him, after all."

"What?"

"Never mind. You just sit tight. We'll get the next flight off the island and be home as soon as—"

"Don't you dare!" Lisa cried. "Don't you dare cut your vacation short because of me. I'd never be able to look you in the face again."

"That's about the dumbest thing I've ever heard you say."

"I'm sorry." Lisa took a deep breath. "I just need some information from someone who knows me."

"Well, of course I know you."

"Do you...can you tell me...am I married?"

An even longer pause this time. "Oh...my...God. You mean it, don't you? You really don't remember."

Chapter Nine

Lisa swallowed so hard she was sure that Belinda could hear it over the phone. "I really don't remember. A man came to the ranch the other day. He said he was Roger Hampton and he was my husband, and he tried to get me to leave with him."

"He *what?*" A string of curses followed. Then, "That creep. That arrogant, overblown piece of frog bait. That bastard! That…that *lawyer.*"

Her last word was delivered with such venom that it surprised a laugh out of Lisa.

"That no good pile of human refuse," Belinda said heatedly, "is your *ex*-husband, and good riddance to bad rubbish."

Lisa swallowed. Her gaze whipped to Jack. "My…my *ex*-husband? I'm divorced?" The relief that flooded her was almost overwhelming.

"You bet your hind end you are, and very happily,

I might add. You divorced him after barely a year of marriage because he cheated on you from the beginning. Now he's trying to coerce you into marrying him again. That's why you came to the ranch, to get away from him.''

With her gaze still locked on Jack, Lisa gripped the phone tighter. ''Oh, God.'' It was coming back. All of it, in huge, solid waves. ''I remember.''

The enormity of the onrush made her stagger. She reached out to catch herself, and Jack was there, steadying her with a hand on her shoulder.

She spoke into the phone, but her words were for Jack. *''I remember.''*

On the other end of the line Belinda let out a loud yell. ''You remember something? What? What?''

Lisa shouted with laughter. ''You, for starters. Oh, Belinda, it's you. I *know* you. I know *me!* I called you. You offered me a place to stay. I remember!''

Jack's hand was still on her shoulder, squeezing gently. Lisa placed her hand over his and returned the pressure.

Jack couldn't take his eyes off her. While she spoke with Belinda, he watched animation light her eyes and curve her lips. She had her memory back and was glowing with it.

He'd wanted her memory to return. He was elated for her. He was especially glad to learn that she wasn't married to Hampton.

Hell, *glad* didn't even come close. The strength of the emotion that swept through him when she'd said *ex*-husband should probably worry him. After all, it shouldn't matter to him, except that naturally he wanted Lisa to be happy, and he didn't see how she could be with the man he'd met the other day.

But he couldn't worry about it just then. It was taking all his willpower to keep from picking her up in his arms and swinging her around the room. Which was not the sort of thing a man ought to do with a woman who was within a month of having a baby. Less than a month now, he realized.

Besides, he was honest enough with himself to admit that he wanted to do more than swing her around the room. More than hold her in his arms. But having been married to a sleeze like Hampton, who would lie to a woman with no memory and try to take advantage of her, Jack wouldn't be surprised if Lisa never wanted anything to do with a man again.

"Are you kidding?" Lisa was saying when Jack finally tuned back in. "You should see me. Basketball be damned. I look like I'm smuggling a giant beach ball."

The two women spoke for several more minutes, then promised each other a good long visit when Belinda and Ace came home at the end of the week.

Lisa turned away from Jack to hang up the phone. She took an inordinate amount of time about it, reluctant to turn back and face him. What would she see in his eyes, and he in hers, now that they both knew she wasn't married?

Maybe she was wrong to hope, but she wanted...oh, damn, she wanted him to want her, but who was she kidding? Single or not, she was as big as a barn and had never felt so unattractive in her life. What would a man like Jack want with a woman like her?

"Lisa?"

She couldn't stand there all night with her back to

him as though she was afraid to face him. She wasn't afraid. Of course she wasn't.

She was terrified.

But she turned around, anyway, because she couldn't stand not knowing for another second.

Neither spoke. They looked at each other, not touching, for a long moment before Jack reached out and pulled her to him. She could read his intention in his eyes. Her heart soared. He was going to kiss her. If he didn't hurry, she feared she might die of wanting.

He lowered his head until his mouth was only a breath away from hers. "I want to kiss you."

"What's stopping you?"

He smiled slightly. "Nothing. Absolutely—" he brushed his lips across hers once "—nothing." Twice.

At the touch of his mouth, Lisa stopped breathing. She wanted more, much more. And then he was giving it to her, softly, relentlessly. He was so gentle, the kiss so tender, she felt her eyes sting as they slid closed.

Moments ago she had regained her memory, but as Jack kissed her, every kiss she'd ever had faded away into nothing. There was only this, only Jack. Only now. Never had anything moved her so much.

He deepened the kiss and she melted. Simply...melted. Kissing Jack was like nothing she'd ever experienced. It was at once a brilliant sunset and a quiet dawn. It sparkled, it shimmered, it devoured her.

The heat surprised her. So did the low growl from Jack's throat.

Oh, my. She had never made a man growl before.

How empowering. How liberating. She threaded her fingers through his hair and silently begged for more.

Jack gave it, and gladly. He'd been holding back, trying not to come on too strong, when what he'd wanted to do was devour her. With her offering, he did.

Now he knew why he'd been drawn to her, why he'd wanted to taste her lips so badly. Something must have been telling him she would go to his head faster than whiskey. He'd known she would taste sweet. He had anticipated the fire she ignited deep inside him.

Hunger and need gripped him, and he tasted both on her lips. Deeper and deeper he took them until he was gasping for breath. And still he kissed her, stroked her tongue with his in a rhythm dictated by the pounding of blood in his loins.

With his hands he explored. Her back was trim, delicate yet strong. When his palms brushed the sides of her breasts and she inhaled sharply, he realized things were about to go too far, and he eased back.

"He was wrong," he whispered fiercely against her lips. He took one last hard taste, then tore his mouth free. "You are *very* good at this."

Breathless, Lisa forced herself to open her eyes and look at him. In his eyes she saw the same intense wonder that she felt. Slowly, she smiled. "So are you."

They stood there in each other's arms, staring at each other and grinning for a long moment without speaking.

Then Jack stroked her cheek with one fingertip and said, "Will you tell me what happened on the phone? Did everything come back to you?"

Still smiling, Lisa tilted her head back and closed her eyes. "Yes. It just came. One minute my past was a blank, the next everything flooded back."

Jack watched her exposed throat as she spoke. It would have taken a stronger man than he to resist. He pressed his lips there, nibbled lightly with his teeth, and was rewarded with Lisa's small needy whimper.

"Oh, Jack," she whispered.

From her throat he kissed and nibbled his way up and over her jaw to her ear. When she shivered, his hands trembled. His hands had never trembled with a woman before. At least not since his first time, when he'd been fifteen.

He wasn't fifteen anymore, but Lisa made him feel all those same hot trembly feelings. He wasn't some fumbling teenager, yet he was close to fumbling. This was Lisa in his arms, and he was a grown man. With as many highs and lows as her emotions had seen during the past week, she was too vulnerable. When he made love to her, he wanted her steady. He wanted her to know what she was doing. He wasn't sure she did just then.

"So tell me…" He took a final taste of her earlobe, then eased back and smiled at her. "Where did you live when you were ten?"

Lisa blinked at his abrupt change of mood. She didn't know whether to punch him for getting her all worked up and then leaving her that way, or be grateful that he hadn't taken them any farther. She settled on grateful.

"The same place I lived from the time I was three until I was eighteen—the state orphanage."

"You said your parents disappeared. You were never adopted?"

"No."

"I...don't know what to say."

"There's nothing to say," she told him. "That's just the way it was. I never knew anything else. I knew there *was* something else. I knew what families were, and I always wanted one." She heaved a sigh. "I need to explain about Roger, but it could take a while. I'm going to have a glass of milk. Would you like me to put on a fresh pot of coffee?"

"I'll do it."

While Jack started the coffee, Lisa poured herself some milk.

"Maybe," she said, "if I hadn't wanted a family so badly, I might not have fallen for Roger's charm."

Jack leaned back against the counter and folded his arms across his chest. His eyes narrowed with skepticism. "Charm?"

"Oh, yes." She sipped her milk and paced the length of the table and back. "Roger can be very charming when he wants to be. I was young—twenty-two. He was twenty-eight. He'd been working as a public defender for a couple of years and had just left there and joined his family's law firm. Very old, very prestigious. And he was...dazzling."

Jack wanted to snort in disgust, but refrained. She wasn't all dreamy-eyed while she was telling him this. There was a note of self-derision in her voice.

"But it was his family I really fell for. He had all these brothers and sisters, aunts and uncles, cousins. There are scads of Hamptons just in the Denver area alone. The first time he took me to meet them, it was

July Fourth. They welcomed me as if I belonged and made me feel a part of them right from the start.''

This time, Jack noted, there was wistfulness in her eyes.

''Oh, I loved his family. I knew if I married him I would finally have the family I'd always wanted. I'm ashamed to say I let them blind me to Roger's true nature.''

Behind Jack the coffee finished brewing. He took a cup from the cabinet and filled it.

Lisa set her glass on the table. With her hands splayed across her abdomen, she took up her pacing again.

''Is she kicking?'' Jack asked.

Lisa smiled briefly. ''No, she's quiet right now. It's me I'm trying to keep calm, but it's not easy when I think about that stunt Roger pulled, showing up here and lying the way he did. I can't *believe* that jerk. I realize now that he didn't claim to be my husband the other day until after he found out I had amnesia. The slime. He knew I wouldn't be able to deny it.''

If she was trying to stay calm, Jack noted, he didn't want to see her riled. Anger sprung rapidly to life across her features.

''His detective must have found me,'' she muttered.

Jack set his coffee cup on the counter. ''His detective?'' he said slowly. She wasn't the only one feeling anger all of a sudden. ''Your ex-husband had you followed by a detective?''

''For months,'' she stated flatly. ''Which is one reason I came here.'' She stopped pacing and put a hand to her forehead. ''Dammit. I can't…I can't remember…''

"Can't remember what?"

She let out a groan of frustration. "I guess there are still holes in my memory. I'm sure I would have checked my rearview mirror to make sure no one was behind me when I turned off at the ranch, but I can't remember doing it. I can't even remember getting here, for that matter."

"Wait a minute. You're so used to being followed that you make a habit of checking your rearview mirror before turning off somewhere? What kind of bastard is Hampton?"

"The royal, card-carrying, certified kind," she said with a snarl. "I was so happily divorced. What in the world was I thinking to let that conniving egomaniac near me again?" She whirled—or she came as close to it as a woman eight months pregnant can—and stomped across the floor and back. "I must have been out of my mind." She took another lap, harder, faster this time. "I should have been committed for even *speaking* to him again." She spun on her heel.

Jack snagged her arm before she could start back across the room. "You're gonna make the kid seasick." He nudged her toward a chair at the table. "Sit. Take a deep breath. Drink some milk."

"Okay." She sat. "You're right." She closed her eyes and took a deep breath, then let it out. "I get worked up when I think about Roger." She took a sip of milk. "He was having me followed. He was showing up everywhere I went. The stress was getting to me. I was afraid..."

"You were afraid of him?" *Let him show up here again, by God, and I'll teach that bastard a lesson he won't soon forget.*

"No, not like you mean. Not for myself, anyway."

"What do you mean?"

She sighed. "Several months ago..." She paused and stroked her belly with both hands. "More than eight. About a year, actually. I ran into Roger at a party one of my clients gave. It was the first time I'd seen him since the divorce three years earlier. I told you he could be charming. He was more than charming that night. He was...disarming. He told me that divorcing him was the smartest thing I'd ever done, that he had deserved every accusation I'd made. When he apologized, he seemed so genuinely sincere. Contrite. And for the first time since the divorce, he asked me to forgive him. I really, really thought he'd changed."

She paused and took another sip, then set the glass down and cupped it in both palms. "You aren't asking what I needed to forgive him for."

Jack didn't want to ask, but he had to know. "I already know he was emotionally abusive. Was he physically abusive, too?"

"No. No, nothing like that. I didn't even understand at the time that he was emotionally abusive. All I knew was that he cheated on me the entire year we were married. I didn't find out about it for a long time, and even then I kept thinking... Well, I guess I wasn't thinking at all. He married me to please his family and expected me to ignore his little outings, as he called them."

"I was right, wasn't I. He told you his cheating was your fault."

"Oh, yeah." She slugged back the last of her milk as if it was a shot of tequila. All she needed was a lime to suck on for the picture to be complete.

"He lied, you know," Jack said, keeping his tone

easy when what he wanted to do was get his hands around Roger Hampton's throat and squeeze.

"Anyway, where was I?" she asked, ignoring Jack's comment.

"Lisa, he lied. It was not your fault."

"Oh, I know that." She lowered her gaze and stared at her empty glass. "It doesn't matter how lousy I was in bed, he still made the decision to cheat on me."

"That's not what I—"

"The night I saw him at the party last year, he asked me to dinner."

Jack ground his teeth together and let her talk. But he wasn't through with the topic of her husband telling her she was lousy in bed. Damn the man.

But what if she was? What if she just lay there like a cold fish?

Jack snorted at the thought.

"Did you say something?"

"No, sorry." He'd meant what he'd told her that night they came home from town and she'd first mentioned Roger. She was the warmest, most loving, most generous woman he'd ever known. If she and her husband had marital problems it certainly wasn't because Lisa was cold or unresponsive. She just wasn't made that way.

"Jack? You look like you're trying to swallow ground glass. If you'd rather not hear this... I'm sorry. I thought—"

"No. I'm sorry. I, uh, made the coffee too strong, that's all. He asked you to dinner?"

She eyed him a moment, then went on. "Yes, he asked me out. When I said no, he said he didn't blame me and wondered if he could ask me again some other time. I was floored. He was being so nice, so reasonable. I thought—hoped—it meant that he'd finally grown up. I thought that maybe working in his family's law firm, with his grandfather around all the time, had matured him.

"Oh, he played me like a fish on a line. He waited a month before calling me, and then it was to ask me to his grandfather's seventieth birthday party. He said his grandfather had been asking about me. God, I was such a sucker."

Jack stood behind her chair and started massaging her shoulders. "Talking about this is making you tense."

She moaned. "Mmm. Kissing's not the only thing you're good at."

He hoped she didn't notice the way his hands tightened abruptly on her shoulders. He'd like to show her a few other things he was good at. "Why, Ms. Hampton, was that a come-on?"

Lisa giggled. "With this shape?" She held her arms out and looked down at her belly. "Not on your life."

"I've told you before, I like your shape."

"Yeah, you called me a cupcake. I'll remember that, Sir Jack. Oh, yes, right there," she said when he hit a particularly tight spot on her shoulder.

The sounds of pleasure she was making were enough to turn Jack's knees to jelly. Yet at the same time, he ached for the story she'd been telling.

"Where was I?" she asked as if reading his mind. "Oh, yeah." Her eyes were closed now and her neck limp, head hanging forward. "I was a sucker."

"I doubt that."

"No, it's true. I really was. I went with him to his

grandfather's birthday party, and then we started dating. I didn't even tell Belinda, because I knew what she'd say. She would have ranted and raved and called me a stupid twit. She would have said that he knew how badly I missed having a family and he was using his to seduce me, and she'd have been right.''

"There's nothing wrong with wanting a family. Sounds pretty normal to me, particularly when you grew up without one.''

"It's not a good enough reason to marry a man. Besides, when people marry because they want a family, it's usually because they want to start a family of their own, not just because they want a bunch of in-laws.''

"You weren't in love with him?''

She sighed. "I thought I was. No, I was. I loved him, and he married me because his grandfather liked me.''

"He didn't love you?''

"Ha. The only time Roger Hampton understands the meaning of the word *love* is when he looks in a mirror. Why I let myself forget that little personality quirk, I'll never know.'' She shifted her shoulders. "You've got to quit that, or I'm going to fall asleep right here at the table. I think I want another glass of milk. Talking about Roger leaves a bad taste in my mouth.''

She started to get up, but Jack whisked her glass away and headed for the fridge. "I'll get it.''

"Thank you. Has anyone ever told you what a nice man you are?''

"Oh, yeah,'' he said, placing her refilled glass before her. "I'm a regular prince. Ask anybody.''

"I don't need to ask. I mean it, Jack,'' she added

sincerely. "I don't know what I would have done without you."

"You'd have done just fine."

"Oh, yeah, like I have such a great track record. I didn't do so fine on my own in Denver, at least not on a personal level. I'd been seeing Roger again for about a month when he called me at work and asked if I wanted to go to a movie that night. I was…well, I was charmed. Again. He'd never taken me to a movie before."

"Never? You lived in a huge city with dozens of theaters and he never took you?"

"He never said, but I got the impression that he felt going to a movie was too…plebeian for someone of his stature."

Jack rolled his eyes and refilled his coffee cup.

"I was late leaving work and Roger was going to pick me up. I rushed home, and when I walked into the house, I surprised a burglar."

"Were you hurt?" Jack demanded instantly.

"No. I was scared to death, though, when he threatened me with my own butcher knife. But Roger burst in and scared the man away."

"At least he was good for something. Did you get a good look at the burglar? Were the police able to catch him?"

"He was masked. Needless to say, I didn't feel much like going to the movie after that little experience. I was so rattled I let Roger pour me a drink. He kept pouring them and one thing led to another, and, well—" she gave Jack a wry grin and patted her belly "—he spent the night."

"Ah."

"Yes. Ah. I was convinced I was falling in love with him again and that he had completely changed."

"But he hadn't?"

"When a snake sheds its skin, it's still a snake. The morning after...well, the morning after, he left his watch on my nightstand. It was the Rolex his grandfather had given him when he passed the bar, so I decided to drop it off to him at his office on my way to work."

She sat there for a long moment and stared off into space. "He was there," she murmured.

"Roger?"

Lisa blinked and cleared her vision. "Roger, and the burglar from the night before."

"The burglar? In Roger's office?"

"I would never have recognized him, but I heard them talking. Roger was counting out a great deal of cash, and the man thanked him, said the next time Roger wanted help scaring a woman into bed, just give him a call."

"Son of a— Roger paid the guy to break into your house and scare you?"

"That's it in a nutshell. We won't go into how that made me feel, but I made this really spectacular scene right there in the law offices." She sipped on her milk. "As it turns out, our divorce was the first divorce in Roger's family—ever, as far as anyone knew. Roger was pushing his grandfather to make him a partner in the law firm, but George—that's his grandfather—told him he wasn't about to have a divorced man as a partner in the firm he'd devoted his life to. So they worked out a deal. If Roger and I remarried, he would get his partnership."

Jack nearly spewed his mouthful of coffee across the table.

"Yeah, that's more or less what I thought, too," Lisa said, noting his reaction. "Roger's been hounding me ever since—particularly once he found out I was pregnant. He wants that partnership in the worst way. He started calling me, leaving messages, sending flowers to my home and office. He even hired that blasted private investigator so he could claim he loved me so much he simply had to know where I was all the time."

"Has he ever heard of *stalking?*" Jack demanded.

"He's heard of it. I've filed more than one complaint with the police."

"They at least slapped him with a restraining order, I hope."

"Are you kidding? His uncle, a judge, took care of making sure that never happened, then sent orders down to his cousin, the police captain, to make sure the courts weren't bothered with any more of my little fairy tales."

"I see why you wanted to get away."

"That, plus the wedding plans were getting to me."

"The *what?*"

"Roger decided months ago that he wasn't going to take no for an answer and started making wedding plans. No one's ever told him no before and made it stick. He's never lost a case in court, never settled, never plea-bargained. He *always* gets his way. He's absolutely convinced that I'll change my mind."

"But that's...that's..."

"Crazy?" she offered. "Preposterous? Outrageous? All of the above. I finally resorted to contacting his grandfather and telling him to call Roger off.''

''Didn't work?''

Lisa shook her head. "He said he wouldn't dream of interfering in our little lovers' spat.''

"They're all certifiable in that family.''

"You won't get an argument out of me. I just hope this poor baby doesn't inherit it,'' she said, rubbing her abdomen. "My doctor agreed that the stress I was under—not from my job, but from Roger—wasn't good for me or the baby, so I decided to get out of town for a while.'' She took another sip of milk. "Oh, good grief!'' she exclaimed.

"What?''

"I just remembered all the stuff in my trunk.''

"The trunk of your car?''

She nodded. "Before tonight I had about decided that I had come up here to have the baby, but I couldn't figure out why I hadn't brought any baby things with me. That seven thousand—*now* I remember. All my financial records are in my briefcase in the trunk of the car. Otherwise I would have found them and realized I hadn't cleaned out my bank accounts to get that much cash.''

Jack's lips twitched. "You mean you really did steal it?''

Lisa grinned. "At least that would be something colorful I could remember from my past, but no, I didn't steal it. When I left town, I stopped at a car lot and sold my car. I cashed the check and took the bus to another car lot where I paid cash for an older car. The seven thousand I had in my purse when I got here is what I had left after the purchase.''

"We'll make a run into town tomorrow afternoon and get your things from your trunk."

"Thank you." She sighed. "It seems I'm always thanking you for something."

"Aw, shucks, ma'am," he said with an exaggerated drawl. "Here at the Flying Ace, we aim to please."

She finished her milk and Jack finished his coffee, and they gravitated toward the living room. Jack led her to the couch and sat down beside her.

"So you really did come here to have your baby?"

"I was afraid Roger might do something really crazy if I stayed in Denver, like steal the baby from the hospital to make me marry him."

"Hell." Jack rubbed a hand over his face. "I hadn't thought of something like that, but it sounds like with him anything's possible."

"That's why I called Belinda. I was so stressed out that I couldn't think straight and didn't trust my own judgment. I was hoping she would come up with a solution. She's the one who said I should come here. When she told me about the section house, I thought of all that privacy, where no one could find me, and it sounded like heaven."

"Until you ended up in the ditch. How did that happen, by the way?"

Lisa frowned. "I don't remember. I remember getting…no, I don't. I think…the last thing I remember before coming to when you found me was leaving Denver. How odd that I can remember everything else, but not coming to Wyoming."

"Not so odd," Jack said. "Didn't the doctor say you might have trouble remembering what happened right before the accident?"

"I guess he did." She grinned. "What can I say? I've had amnesia. I forgot."

He smiled at her. "How does it feel, having your memory back?"

"You're kidding, right?"

"I guess that was a dumb question."

His look, just a little on the sheepish side, inexplicably pleased Lisa. "It feels liberating. Like I've stepped out of the shadows and into the light. How hokey is that?"

"Not hokey." Jack held her gaze and shook his head. "I can't tell you how glad I am that everything's all right now."

"Everything but good ol' Roger," she said with disgust.

"Yeah, good ol' Roger." Jack frowned and scratched his jaw. "What are we gonna do about him?"

"He's not your problem, Jack."

"Let's see." With his hands behind his head, Jack slouched down on the couch until his neck rested against the back and he could study the ceiling. "There's stalking. We have our own judges in Wyoming," he added casually. "In fact, we even have one in the family, so to speak. Two can play that game."

"There's a Judge Wilder? I thought you were all ranchers."

"Well, he's not exactly a Wilder. He's my sister's stepson's late mother's father's cousin."

Lisa blinked in astonishment. "You made that up."

"Couldn't. My imagination's not that good. But now that I think about it, Rachel is adopting Cody, so he's not her stepson anymore—he's her son. Anyway, if that judge doesn't see things our way, there are others. As for Hampton, he came to the ranch and presented himself under false pretenses and tried to get you to leave with him, knowing you didn't know who he was. I wonder if that could be considered attempted kidnapping.''

Lisa stared at him in awe. ''Why do I get the feeling you're not joking?''

He raised his head and looked at her. ''Because I'm not. If we don't do something about Roger, you'll be looking over your shoulder the rest of your life. What happens when you want to leave the baby at day care someday? What's to keep him from snatching her then?''

While it warmed her heart to hear Jack say ''we'' and refer to her baby as ''her,'' it chilled her to realize he had a legitimate point. She had to find a way to make Roger leave her and the baby alone.

''It's not your problem, Jack.''

''You're not in this alone,'' he told her solemnly.

She closed her eyes, half in frustration, half in uncertainty. ''I have to stand on my own.''

Jack reached out and took her hand in his. ''You can stand on your own without having to stand by yourself.''

Lisa was more touched than she could say. ''I guess I have to say it again.''

''Say what?''

''Thank you.'' Never had anyone been so generous with her, so giving of himself. She couldn't bring herself to think that he was merely setting her up for a fall, the way Roger would have, or that he only wanted something from her. Not Jack.

Suddenly he burst out laughing.

As moved as she had been, his laughter came as a crushing blow. She looked away quickly to hide the sudden moisture gathering in her eyes. What a fool she'd been to think he'd been sincere. Men weren't sincere. Hadn't she learned that over and over from Roger?

"Hey," Jack said, placing a finger under her chin and turning her face toward him. "Lisa?"

She jerked her face from his touch. "I'm glad I can be such an easy source of amusement for you." She pushed herself away from the back of the couch and started to rise.

"Whoa." Jack grasped her arm and kept her from standing up. "What the hell are you talking about? You're mad that I laughed because the front of your blouse moved all by itself?"

With her tears swallowed back, irritation set in. Irritation with herself. She'd known, oh, she'd *known* better than to let any tender feelings develop for a man, to trust a man. Didn't she always get kicked in the teeth, metaphorically speaking? Didn't she always— "My blouse?"

He looked at her cautiously. "What did you think I was laughing at?"

"You were laughing at my blouse?"

Frowning, he gave a slight shrug. "The baby must have moved. One little spot of your blouse over your stomach just suddenly poked out, then fell back down." His voice trailed away, then he asked again, "What did you think I was laughing at?"

Lisa felt like a fool. She had thought for years that men made fools of women, but she was discovering that she apparently needed no help in that department. She could make a fool of herself all on her own.

Her eyes stung again. How incredibly unfair of her to lay Roger's shortcomings on Jack's shoulders! How long had she been doing that?

"Talk to me, cupcake."

"I'm sorry." Tears nearly choked her. Tears of shame. She buried her face in her hands. "I'm s-sorry."

"No."

Oh, God, now he would be disgusted by her tears and would—

You're doing it again!

This wasn't Roger. It was Jack. Yet ever since her memory had returned, she seemed to be having trouble keeping them separate in her mind, and that was so unfair. To Jack, and to herself.

"I'm s-sorry," she said again.

Then, incredibly, the next thing she knew she was being lifted and turned until she sat on Jack's lap with his arms, those strong warm arms, wrapped securely around her.

Jack didn't know what was going on. All he knew was that somehow he had hurt her, yet *she* was apologizing to *him* and now she was crying and he couldn't stand it. "Don't cry," he begged as he held her on his lap. "I'm the one who's sorry. Don't be hurt, honey. Don't let me hurt you. That's the last thing on earth I'd ever want to do."

Lisa sniffed and took a swipe at her cheeks. "You didn't hurt me. *I* hurt me. And I hurt you, too, but you didn't even know it."

"I knew it. The minute I saw your tears. That hurts me, because I can't stand to see you unhappy."

A certain look in her eyes—guilt? shame?—

brought a new ache to Jack. "It's him, isn't it? Something I did reminded you of him."

"It's not your fault," she said in a rush. "I'm just not used to a man who isn't trying to make fun of me or use me or get something from me. You don't want anything from me. I had no right to think that of you. I know you're not like him."

"You're damn right I'm not." He cupped her damp cheek in his palm. "I'm nothing like him. If I could, I'd burn the memory of him right back out of your head. But if you think I don't want anything from you, then you're forgetting this." And he kissed her. Gently at first, then deeply, passionately, as if she were a feast and he was starving.

Lisa was initially stunned, then lost. His hunger became hers. She clutched at his shoulders to bring him closer and gave herself to the kiss. To him. If their last kiss had been overwhelming, this one was...devastating.

His hands, those callused workingman's hands, were both gentle and fierce at the same time, and they were everywhere. He stroked her back, her arms, her abdomen. When he cupped her breast, everything inside her focused there. It was the most exquisite thing she'd ever felt.

"Oh, Jack," she breathed against his mouth.

"Tell me no."

"I can't," she whispered.

He kissed her again. "Tell me to stop." And again.

"Don't stop."

Her words were sweet, sweet music to his ears, but he knew he should call a halt. "I'm not what you need," he told her.

"You're exactly what I need."

He looked into her eyes and knew she believed it, but he couldn't let her. "Then I'm not what you deserve. You deserve a man who can make promises he'll keep forever, a man who'll love you. If I had that in me to give a woman, you would be that woman, but I don't, Lisa. I can give you pleasure, friendship, affection, but—"

"Hush." She placed her fingers over his lips. "We're a good pair, then, aren't we? You can't love a woman, and I don't want to love a man."

Jack pressed his forehead against hers and held her close. It must have been a cruel twist of fate, he decided, that made her feel so right in his arms, as if she belonged there forever, as if his reason for existing was to hold her.

"Then we should stop." He hated saying the words, but knew he had to. Still, he couldn't stop himself from kissing her cheek, her nose, her jaw.

"I don't want to stop. But…"

"But what?"

Lisa looked at him and swallowed hard. "I'm afraid I'll disappoint you. I'm not any good at this. And I look like a whale."

"I told you," Jack said, brushing his thumb over her nipple and capturing her gasp with his mouth. "I like the way you look, and you're *very* good at this. Can't you feel what you do to me?" He nudged his hips against her to show her exactly what he meant.

Lisa felt his erection press against her. She couldn't doubt that he wanted her. And she wanted him. All she could do was hold on and hope that it would be as good between them when they made love as it was now. Because the one thing she knew was that she couldn't pass up this chance to be with Jack. She needed his closeness, his strength, his touch. His warmth and laughter. His belief in her.

"Take me to bed, Jack."

Her request humbled him. She had to have reservations. She'd already said she was afraid she would disappoint him. Yet once again she proved her courage by asking this of him. Maybe he should say no. Maybe he should stop this before it went any further, but he couldn't. For himself it was the last thing in the world he wanted to do. And he would be damned if he would do anything to add to the feelings of inadequacy her ex-husband had instilled in her.

Against her lips he whispered, "It will be my—" he paused to nibble once, twice "—extreme pleasure." Then he gave, and took, a deeper kiss, with tongues dancing and hearts pounding.

Lisa nearly wept in relief. Never had she knowingly taken such a gamble. But once again Jack proved how different he was from Roger by not making her beg, not patting her on the head and telling her she didn't know what she wanted. Not outright laughing at her.

No, this was Jack, who took such gentle care with her and made her feel good about herself. Jack, who made her burn deep down inside in a way she never had before. Jack, who with a single kiss could melt her bones.

"Hold on to me," he murmured.

"Yes." *For as long as I can.*

Chapter Ten

He carried her upstairs and stood her beside her bed.

"I think I'm nervous," she said.

Jack swallowed. "Me, too." He ran his hands up and down her arms, aching to feel her flesh but determined to go slowly.

"You?" she asked.

"I've never made love with a pregnant woman before." He splayed one hand over her stomach. "She'll be all right, won't she, if we're careful?"

Right then Lisa would have walked through fire for Jack Wilder. "She'll be fine."

"Do you mind if I turn on the lamp?" Jack asked.

If she could have thought of a way to see him in the dark, she would have said no, that she wanted the light off. But she desperately wanted to see him. If that meant he would be able to see her, she would try not to think about it. Instead of answering, she turned to the nightstand and switched on the lamp herself. The room filled with a soft buttery glow.

"But I warn you," she told him nervously, "what you're about to see is not a pretty sight."

"If you're talking about this," he said placing his hand over her belly again, "I'll have to disagree. I've told you that before."

Yes, he had told her before that she wasn't fat, that her extra bulk was caused by the miracle of life. That he liked the way she looked. Still, he had yet to see her without her clothes. He might yet change his mind. But when he started kissing her again, she forgot to worry about what his reaction might be.

"You might not like what you see beneath my clothes, either," he said.

"Oh—" she undid the first button on his shirt "—I can pretty much guarantee I will."

"I hope so." He let her continue unbuttoning his shirt while he nibbled his way across her face and down her neck. "I want to please you. I want to make you feel all the things I feel when you kiss me."

Lisa's fingers fumbled at every nibble. Maybe it wouldn't matter that she wasn't any good at this. He seemed to be good enough for both of them. And she had a feeling she was soon going to be extremely grateful for that.

"There's another reason I call you cupcake." With both hands he stroked gently down to her breasts, then over her abdomen. "Because I can't wait to peel you out of your wrapping and gobble you up."

Who would have thought, Lisa wondered, that talk of cupcakes could make a woman's knees turn to water?

Jack caught her as she swayed against him, and

then he did what he'd been wanting to do. He peeled off her shirt and felt her bare flesh beneath his fingers. It was every bit as soft and silky as he'd imagined. Her bra was pale blue lace, almost too pretty to be covered up all the time. He had no trouble getting it off her.

"So beautiful," he whispered, stroking the peaks of her breasts.

Lisa sucked in a sharp breath. The sensation of his fingers on her nipples struck tingling heat straight to her core. His name left her lips on a breath. Then the room spun and the floor tilted away. It took her a moment to realize that Jack had picked her up in his arms and was taking them both down onto the bed.

In seconds he had shed her of the rest of her clothes. He did it so fast and so easily that there was no time for her to be embarrassed or self-conscious before he was stroking her bare belly.

"This is…amazing. It's harder, firmer than I expected. And your skin—it's so delicate to begin with, it's a miracle it can stretch so much. Does it hurt?"

He was so sweetly, wonderfully absorbed in her belly that Lisa felt her heart turn over. "No, it doesn't hurt."

"She's quiet in there." He bent down and pressed his lips to the spot just below her navel. "You just sleep in here, you hear? You're too young for what your mama and I are about to do."

Lisa smiled while her eyes misted over. He would make such a wonderful father—if only he would let himself love a woman. He said it was because he simply didn't have it in him. He thought he wasn't capable of that kind of love. But he was wrong. She wished she knew a way to convince him, but then it might sound as if she was trying to talk him into loving *her*. She couldn't do that to him. He trusted her with knowledge that was personal and private. She could not, would not do anything to make him think she might betray that trust. Just as he wouldn't betray the trust she'd given him by confessing that she was a failure at satisfying a man. He hadn't believed her any more than she believed him.

When he took off his shirt and she pressed her hands against that hard-muscled chest, he made a sound deep in his throat, half growl, half groan, that sent a rush of pleasure through her almost as great as when he stroked her. As they touched each other, learned each other's shapes and textures, he let her know in a dozen different ways that he very much liked her touch.

And she liked his. He made her feel things she'd never felt before. Such pleasure, such joy. With words and touches, kisses and small love bites that shot jolts of electricity through her, he loved her, encouraged her. For the first time in her life Lisa reveled in the sheer power and excitement of being a woman.

But she wanted more. She wanted it all, wanted him inside her. "Jack."

"Yes."

She was gratified to realize that he was as breathless as she.

"Like this," he added. He rolled to his back and lifted her astride his hips.

"Oh…" She didn't wait, couldn't. "Yes." With her hands braced on his chest, she lowered herself and took him in.

Jack held his breath against the need to slam into her, but this was too good to rush. As he looked up at her rising above him, her face tense with pleasure, her full gorgeous breasts filling his hands, her womb expanded with the miracle of life, he knew he'd never seen anything more beautiful or more erotic in his life.

Then she lifted herself up slowly, so slowly, and slid back down. Then again. And again. Until he thought he might die of sheer ecstasy. That wasn't a word he normally used, but it was the only word in his mind when he felt her inner muscles contract as she shot over the edge.

His control snapped. He gripped her hips and thrust up so hard and high that his back came off the mattress. He thought he cried out her name as he pumped his life force into her, but his mind shut down, so he couldn't be sure. It didn't matter. Only the pleasure mattered, and the woman who so generously shared it with him.

Lisa lay on her side where she had collapsed, half on, half off Jack. If she didn't move, he was going to feel the tears she couldn't seem to stop.

"No," he said when she tried to push away. "Don't—you're crying." He eased her onto her back and raised over her. "What's wrong. Did I hurt you? Is it the baby?"

"No, no," she said in a rush. "Nothing's wrong. I'm sorry. Nothing's ever been more right. I mean that, Jack. I don't know why I'm crying." But she did know. She was crying because she knew now, without a shadow of a doubt, that she had done the unthinkable. She had fallen in love with him.

"Well, then." He nuzzled her cheeks and sipped

the moisture away. "I guess you know this means I won the argument, hands down."

At his smug teasing tone, she sniffed away the last of her tears. "What argument?"

"The one about whether or not you're any good at this."

Lisa smiled. "I guess I was, huh?"

An intense look came into his eyes. "If you were any better, I don't think I would have survived."

Twice more they made love. Sometime during the night Jack must have turned off the lamp, for when Lisa awoke, the room was dark. The glowing numbers on the digital bedside clock told her it was nearly three in the morning.

The night had been a revelation to Lisa. She'd never dreamed she was capable of that kind of un-inhibited response to a man. Never dreamed a man could be so gentle, yet sometimes fierce with it.

She'd never dreamed, even during those first heady days with Roger, before their troubles began, that she could love a man so deeply that she ached with it.

He slept beside her now, his breathing deep and even, his strong arms enveloping her in warmth and security. "Oh, Jack," she whispered. "You're so wrong about yourself. You are the most loving man I've ever dreamed of. I love you."

But Jack wasn't asleep. When she'd started talking, he had almost answered her. Then, as she went on, he was incapable of answering. She couldn't mean what she'd said. She couldn't love him. Not really.

But what if she did? If ever there was a woman he might be willing to take a chance on, a woman who could teach him how to love, it was this one curled up in his embrace.

It would never work. She couldn't afford to gamble her future, her happiness, the welfare of her child, on whether or not he learned what it was to love a woman.

He could promise her loyalty. She would never have to worry about other women. He could promise her security, and more nights like tonight. He could make her laugh, keep her warm, take care of her and her child. He could give her his name, his home, his family. He could give her more children. He could give her everything he was, everything he had inside him.

Would those things be enough for Lisa if he never found that illusive love inside himself to give her? Or would she one day grow discontent to live without the love she deserved?

The deeper her breathing grew, the greater his confusion. What was he supposed to do—let her walk out of his life?

When he thought of the future, he couldn't imagine it without her. And that terrified him. Because she would leave him. Even though she thought she loved him, she would leave him. She wasn't looking for a permanent man in her life; she'd said so often enough. The women in his life always left him.

Lisa awoke with the sun streaming in through the window. That she was alone in her bed did not surprise her—he had a ranch to run, after all, and couldn't loll around in bed all morning. But she couldn't help the ache that formed around her heart at waking up without him. It was a crippling ache, for she knew that Jack didn't return her feelings. Yet it was a good ache, because it felt absolutely wonderful to be in love.

Now all she had to do was find a way to survive— if she couldn't convince Jack to trust her with his heart.

None of the men were coming in for lunch. Jack had left her a note saying they would all be out repairing fences and not to expect them until supper. He had addressed the note to Cupcake. Lisa held it to her heart and smiled. Never mind the dull ache in her lower back. She felt as if she could dance on air. It was amazing what a few good orgasms could do for a woman.

But now that she had an entire day to herself, she intended to clean the house. Belinda and her family were due back in two days, and Lisa thought of her earlier resolve. She wanted them to find the place as clean when they returned as it was when they left.

She gathered a few cleaning supplies from the pantry and carried them out into the kitchen. She set them on the counter next to the sink, then turned—and stifled a shriek.

"Hello, Lisa."

Her heart jumped right up into her throat. "Roger. How did you get in?"

"I hope you don't mind. The back door was unlocked."

"So you just let yourself into someone else's house?"

"I'm sorry. I missed you so much I couldn't stay away any longer."

Lisa nearly choked. He was putting on his sincere

act, obviously thinking she still suffered from amnesia. She wondered just how far he would go.

"Please say you're ready to come home with me, darling. I can't bear the thought of going home without you. Shall I help you pack?"

"I'm not going anywhere with you."

"Oh, but you must, sweetheart. You have no idea how lonely I've been these past days without you. If not for your amnesia, I know you would have been desolate without me. I can't tell you how sorry I am that it took me so long to get here."

Lisa had heard enough. With a sarcastic smile, she started clapping.

Roger blinked in confusion. "What are you doing?"

"Applauding your performance. You won't win any Oscars with it, but someone who doesn't know you might buy it for a few minutes."

His gaze sharpened. There was recognition in her eyes. She knew him now.

The temperature wasn't quite forty, but Jack had managed to work up a sweat wrestling with stubborn wire torn down by a herd of elk. With his hands occupied, he turned his head and wiped his forehead against his shoulder, then rubbed at the nagging itch on his left ear.

"What's eating you?" Trey demanded.

Jack grunted and took another hitch with the come-along to stretch the wire tighter. "Nothing's eating me."

"The hell you say. Hold it there." Trey held a staple in place over the wire and hammered it into the fence post. "One minute you're all dopey-eyed and grinning like a possum in the corn crib, the next you look like you just ruined your best boots."

"You're imagining things."

"Hmm." Trey hammered in another staple. He knew a man with woman trouble when he saw one. "So how's Lisa?"

"What do you mean?" Jack snapped.

Trey nearly laughed out loud. "Nothing. Just asking. Has she remembered anything else yet? Anything about that guy who showed up claiming to be her husband?"

Jack grunted again.

Trey noted that there'd been a lot of that going on this morning.

"Ex-husband," Jack muttered.

"What?"

"He's her *ex*-husband."

"She remembered that?"

Jack scratched his ear again. "She remembered everything. Just *boom,* and it all came back to her. Damnedest thing."

"Hold that there." Trey stapled the wire to the next post, the one nearest Jack. "Okay, ease off. I'm taking a break."

"Come on, we'll never get finished if you keep taking breaks," Jack complained.

Trey taunted him with a grin. "In a hurry to get back to the house, are you?"

Jack's only answer was a snarl. Wiping his forehead with the back of his gloved hand, he headed for the jug of water in his rig.

"So, she's not married, huh?"

"No," Jack replied tersely.

Trey chuckled. "Oh, I like this, bro. You find out

she's not married, then you start acting all strange. Yep, I'd have to say you're hooked.''

"What do you mean, hooked?"

"Okay, pop-quiz time. Do you think about her all the time?"

Jack frowned. "Maybe."

"Maybe?"

"Some."

"Some?"

"All right, damn you, yes, I think about her all the time. So what?"

"Do you make up excuses to go see her?"

Jack just glared at him.

Trey whooped. "I'll take that as a yes. Does your heart pound when you're around her?"

Jack's gaze narrowed.

"Uh-huh. When you kiss her—you *have* kissed her, haven't you? Never mind. You've kissed her. Does she make your knees go weak?"

"Low blood sugar. That's all it was."

"Low blood sugar, my aunt Fanny."

"You don't have an aunt Fanny."

"You're in love, big brother. And bite me on the nose if it's not the real thing this time. You've got that same dopey look in your eyes that Ace has had ever since Belinda showed up."

Trey's words startled any response right out of Jack. His heart began to beat triple time. Could it be true? Could he really be in love with Lisa?

"No."

"No, what?" Trey demanded. "It's not something you decide. It just happens."

"So says the world's expert on love, right?"

"Hey, I know it when I see it in other people. You

knew it about Ace and Belinda before they did. Why can't I know it about you?''

"Forget it. I don't have what it takes to love a woman the way Ace loves Belinda.''

"What kind of bull is that? You just never met the right woman before, that's all.''

Jack opened his mouth, but nothing came out. Could it be that simple? Could he simply have been waiting all these years to find the one woman he trusted enough? The one woman who would truly, sincerely love him back?

"Well, hell…'' Trey said with trepidation.

"What?''

"I just realized you've been scratching your ear for about the last ten minutes.'' Trey looked out over the range toward headquarters five miles away as if trying to see whatever it was that was wrong that, inexplicable as it was, made Jack's ear itch. "Was Stoney feeling all right this morning?''

Jack barely heard him. Everything inside him shut down and filled with dread. *"Lisa!"*

Jack whipped out his cell phone, but knew what he'd see on the screen as he did. The screen read No Service. They were in a hollow where the signal didn't reach.

For the first time in either of their lives, Jack and Trey left their tools and equipment lying on the ground. Trey barely made it into the rig before Jack hit the gas. Small rocks, grass, mud and slush from the melting snow flew from beneath the tires.

Jack swore under his breath and tried to tell himself he was overreacting. It didn't help. He didn't care if she had merely stubbed her toe, but something was wrong. All he could think of was the baby. And the fact that it was too damned early. What if their love-making last night had harmed the baby? Jack would never forgive himself.

The terrain simply would not permit him to drive fast enough to suit him until he cleared the pasture and made it to the road. Hell, they were all the damn way on the other damn side of the damn ranch. It would take forever to get home.

"It was all an act," Roger accused.

"It wasn't an act. I did have amnesia," Lisa told him. "But the doctor was right—it cleared up on its own. I want you to leave now."

Roger saw his best chance slip through his fingers. If he could have gotten her home and safely married before her memory returned, he'd have had it made. Now it was too late for that, but he still refused to give up. There was more than just a partnership in the firm at stake, and she knew it, the bitch. His entire future was on the line.

For months he'd played the fool for her, trying to convince her to marry him again. She had rebuffed him at every turn, yet he had persisted. He hadn't known how he was going to change her mind, he'd only known that he must. So he'd started planning their wedding. He'd wanted her willing, even if pressured.

Now he would take her any way he could, and civility be damned. Because if he didn't get his hands on the extra quarter of a million dollars that came as a bonus with the partnership, he was a dead man. He was in too deep with the gambling syndicate. They weren't the type of organization that would send him a polite past-due notice.

No, first they would break his thumbs. The next time they would get serious.

Lisa was going to save him from that.

"I'm leaving, all right." He grabbed her by the arm. "And so are you."

Stunned that he would actually lay hands on her, Lisa tried to jerk free, but his hold was too tight. It felt as though his fingers were pressing all the way to the bone in her forearm. "Let go of me!" she cried. "Roger, you're hurting me!"

"I'm going to do a lot more than hurt you if you don't come with me peacefully and do what I tell you." He pulled a notepad and pen from his inside jacket pocket and tossed it onto the table in front of her.

Lisa had a brief flash of hysteria. Only Roger would show up for a kidnapping in an Italian suit, complete with notepad and a two-hundred-dollar fountain pen.

Then sanity returned and she glared her hatred at him. "If you think I'm going anywhere with you, you're out of your mind. You'll never get away with this, Roger. You can't make me marry you."

"That's up to you, of course. I can always simply kill you and forge the marriage license. So tragic, they'll all say. They finally found their way back to each other, and with their first child on the way, when some stranger shot her." He slipped a small chrome pistol from the pocket of his slacks and let it dangle threateningly at his side. "Or maybe I'll just drug you. What a nice docile wife you'll make."

Lisa's blood turned to ice in her veins. Terror locked the breath in her throat. He meant it. The truth was in his eyes. He would kill her.

She swung at him with her fist. Pain shot up her arm. Blood sprayed from his nose.

"You bitch!" He backhanded her across the cheek. "One more move and I'll hit you in that grotesque mound you call a belly."

"No!" She covered her abdomen with her free arm. "You wouldn't hurt your own child."

"I'll do whatever I have to do." He aimed the gun at her stomach.

Dear God, he must have lost his mind. She'd never been afraid of him before. But now, standing in the Wilders' kitchen, she found herself looking into the eyes of a madman and was terrified.

Roger dictated the note and, with a hand that shook despite her best efforts to conceal her fear, Lisa wrote. Then he dragged her out the front door toward his waiting BMW.

They were halfway down the walk toward the car when Stoney, whistling "Sweet Betsy from Pike," came around the corner of the house carrying a bucket of eggs. He stopped and eyed Roger, and the way Roger held her arm.

"Miss Lisa?"

Roger maintained his grip on her and made sure she saw him slip his hand into the pocket that held his gun.

Oh, God, she couldn't let anything happen to Stoney, but maybe there was a way to let him know something was wrong.

"Everything all right?" Stoney asked her.

"Sure, Stoney. This is my husband, Roger. He's taking me home." Her knees were knocking and her heart thundered. The wind sliced through her and made her shiver. "I'm sorry I didn't get to make that ham like I promised, but there's plenty of that shrimp casserole left over from last night. All you have to do is heat it up.''

''But—''

Roger cut him off. ''We have to go, Lisa.'' He tugged on her arm, pulling her down the sidewalk.

''Goodbye, Stoney,'' she called. ''Give my best to your wife.''

With narrowed eyes, Stoney watched them climb into the car and pull away from the house. Something was wrong. Bad wrong. Miss Lisa never made them any shrimp casserole. They'd had ham last night, best ham he'd ever had. And what was that business about his wife? Miss Lisa knew he didn't have a wife.

Lordy, lordy, something was bad wrong, and he'd best be finding Jack and letting him know about it.

Jack and Trey were working on the north fence. That meant Stoney was the only one around. He would just go back to the bunkhouse and call Jack on that fancy cell phone of his and let him know something curious was up.

But just then things got curiouser. The driveway that led to the front of the house, where that fancy black car had been parked, circled back on itself and came out onto the main drive. From there, to leave the ranch, you turned right. That wasn't what the black car did.

Inside that black car Lisa was trying to think of any way she could to keep her and her baby safe, but she knew that if Roger got her away from the Flying Ace, neither of them would ever be safe again. If he got her all the way to Denver—provided he didn't kill her en route—she would never be free of him.

It was easy to tell herself that he couldn't drug her

without her cooperation, but she knew better. She had to eat. Slipping something into her food would be all too easy. She had to sleep. He could inject a drug into her before she could stop him.

Dear God, what was she going to do? She had to keep Roger on the ranch and give Jack time to find her.

That Jack would come for her she had no doubt. Stoney would find him and tell him something was wrong. The man was old, but he was smart, and he knew as well as she did what they'd had for supper the night before.

When Roger hit the end of the circle driveway and started to turn right toward the county highway, Lisa thought fast. "Don't go that way."

"Shut up."

"All right."

Roger hit the breaks so hard Lisa's shoulder strap was the only thing that kept her from bouncing into the dash.

"Why do you not want me to turn right?" he demanded.

More shaken than she'd ever been in her life—even more than the night she'd stumbled upon the knife-wielding "burglar" in her home last year—Lisa struggled to concentrate. She couldn't let him know how terrified she was. That would just become another weapon he would be able to use against her.

"Go ahead," she told him. "In fact, please do. This ridiculous farce will be over that much sooner. We'll meet the rest of the men coming back from town."

"If we run into anyone, you just wave and I'll keep driving."

She managed a nod. "Whatever you say."

He licked his lips nervously. That scared Lisa more than anything. She had never seen Roger nervous. Never seen him anything but completely self-assured.

"What's to the left? And don't lie to me, or I'll make you sorry."

She was already sorry. Sorrier than she could say about ever having met Roger Hampton. Except for the baby he'd given her. The baby he was threatening. The baby that was worth everything to her.

Roger gripped her already bruised arm and shook her. "Answer me."

Lisa winced. "If you go left, you'll find another road about two miles from here that veers off to the left. It cuts through some rocks and ravines and angles south."

God, she'd done it now, she thought as Roger turned left. The side road was there just as she'd described it, but it led only to the family cemetery. What she would do when Roger figured that out, she had no idea. She was praying that Jack would come after her, but it might take a long time for Stoney to find him, then for Jack to find her.

Jack, please come. Please, Jack.

Jack barreled through the back door of the house frantically calling Lisa's name, praying he was mistaken and that nothing was wrong.

"Lisa!"

No answer. He ran upstairs and searched every room. "Lisa! Lisa, answer me."

The house was empty. He raced back downstairs, more frantic than ever. Where could she have gone?

"Jack!" Trey called from the kitchen.

"Did you find her?"

"She— There's a note."

Jack took the piece of paper from Trey and felt the blood drain from his head.

"Jack," it began, "I've gone home with my husband, where I belong. I'll let you know where to send my things."

Yes, he realized, her clothes and things had still been in her room upstairs.

For a second, no longer than that, he believed it. She had left him. When he finally thought he'd found the one woman he could trust, to whom he could give his heart, with whom he could share his life, she—

Then he swore. She wouldn't. She wouldn't do that.

"Hey, man," Trey said. "I'm real sorry, Jack."

Jack swore again. "She despised that bastard. She would never willingly go anywhere with him."

"Then what…"

New fear gripped Jack by the throat. "He took her."

"*Kidnapped* her?"

Stoney banged through the back door. "There you are. We got trouble. Miss Lisa left, but she was actin' awful funny, talkin' about shrimp and wives and all. I tried to call you, but you musta been down—"

"What about Lisa?" Jack demanded. "When did she leave? What did she say? Was she all right?"

"She said we should heat up last night's shrimp for our supper."

Jack nearly exploded in frustration. "I don't give a damn about supper! What did she say about why she was leaving?"

"Jack," Trey interrupted. "we didn't have shrimp last night. We had ham."

"So she was confused. Rattled."

Trey held Jack's gaze. "She's never fixed us shrimp. She wasn't rattled that much. Remember Stoney's joke the first night she cooked for us, about never fixing shrimp casserole? My money says she knew exactly what she was saying."

Stoney scratched the side of his nose. "That's the way I figure it. An' she said I was to tell my wife goodbye for her."

"Your..." Jack squeezed his eyes shut. "Okay, she was trying to tell you something was wrong." He headed for the door. "How long ago did they leave? Was he still driving that black BMW?"

"All I know is that it was shiny and black. Looked new. Left about five minutes ago. And that was real curious," he added.

Jack was halfway out the door. "What was curious about it?" he demanded.

"They headed west."

"What? Are you sure?"

"I know east from west. They headed west. I already called the sheriff," Stoney added as Jack disappeared out the door.

"Damn." Trey ran after his brother, but he was too late this time. Before he could catch up, Jack had jumped in the rig and was tearing out, headed west.

Chapter Eleven

Lisa slowed Roger down as much as she could, telling him that she wasn't sure where the turnoff was and that passing it and having to turn around would waste time. Less than a half mile from the house there was no need for her to slow him down. The road did that for her.

It had been plowed days ago, but with all the snow melting and running across it, the unpaved dirt road was as muddy as a bog and full of deep ruts left by the ranch vehicles. Roger had to drive at a creep. If he didn't, the car slid on the slick mud. If he fell into the ruts, the BMW, much closer to the ground than the four-wheel-drive rigs that used this road, would bottom out.

But her heart was racing and her mouth was dry. A hundred yards ahead the road dipped, and there

•

they would find the turnoff that led to the cemetery. *What then? What then?*

She had no idea.

"You knew this road was impassable. You told me to come this way on purpose."

"I haven't been out of the house in days. How would I know what shape the road is in? All I did was keep you from running into the rest of the ranch hands."

"And I have to ask myself why you did that. For someone who had to be coerced into coming with me, you're being awfully helpful."

Coerced? It was all she could do not to scream at him. She hadn't been coerced. Her life and that of her baby had been threatened. "I just want to get back to Denver and get this wedding over with."

"You're going to do it?" When he looked at her, the car swerved toward the two-foot pile of snow alongside the road, left there by the plow and not yet melted.

"Look out!" she cried.

Roger jerked the steering wheel and the car went into a skid and fishtailed on the slick mud. He slammed on the brakes, but by then the car was going sideways, so the antilock brakes didn't help. The rear end of the car slid and took out a ten-foot strip from the snow piled alongside the road before the back tires sank into the thick mud and the car refused to budge.

Roger swore viciously. Sweat beaded his brow as he gunned the engine. The tires spun. The car only rocked slightly forward and back, forward and back, while the tires turned uselessly in the mud.

•

"You stupid bitch," he snarled. "This all your fault."

"What?" Inside she was trembling, but she clenched her fists in her lap and played it cool. "I was minding my own business, cleaning house. This little trip was your idea."

"Your advice to come this way may end up costing you more than you can afford, *darling*."

She didn't mistake his meaning. He had long since gone over the edge. He would kill her if he had to. She couldn't just sit there and wait for him to do it. But her chances were next to zero even if she got out of the car. There was no way she could outrun him, let alone a bullet.

Dear God, what was she going to do? *Jack! Help me, Jack!*

Roger looked back down the road they had traveled and started swearing again.

Lisa followed his gaze and nearly cried in relief. It was Jack! As if she had conjured him up, there he was, driving his mud-spattered rig so fast it seemed to barely touch the surface of the road.

She reached for the door handle to get out.

Roger grabbed her. She knew, without looking, but she turned her head slowly and looked anyway—straight into the barrel of that nasty little pistol. He held it low, so it couldn't be seen unless someone was right at the window looking in, but it was nonetheless deadly in its aim at her abdomen.

"Here's how it's going to be, Lisa." His breath was coming fast. Sweat glistened across his face. Panic danced a jitterbug in his eyes. "You're going to convince him that you're coming with me by choice. I don't care how you do it, just make him pull us out of this mud so we can get out of here. If you do a good job, I promise I'll divorce you within the next five years and you can keep the kid. If you screw this up..."

"If I screw this up, what?" she hissed. "Are you going to kill me in front of a witness?"

"No. I'm going to kill him."

A deep shudder ripped through her as ice formed in the pit of her stomach. She swallowed and glanced down the road again. Jack was slowing to a stop only yards away.

"It's going to be hard to convince him if he sees that gun," she warned shakily.

"He won't see it, but I'll have my hand on it every second until we're out of here. And don't mistake its small size. It kills just as well as a bigger gun."

He dragged her across the leather seat and out the driver's-side door with him. They sank almost ankle-deep in mud. Roger kept a hold on her arm and stood slightly behind her. His right hand was in his pants pocket. On the gun.

Jack climbed out of his rig.

Never had anything looked so good to Lisa as Jack did just then. God, how she loved him! She wanted to shout at him to get back in, to leave, fast, so he wouldn't get hurt. But the tightening of Roger's fingers around her upper arm silenced her.

Only now did she realize how cold it was. Roger hadn't even let her get her coat, and suddenly she was shivering.

"Looks like you folks have a little problem here," Jack said lazily as he approached. "Is everybody all right?"

"We're fine," Roger told him. "I'm sorry we

couldn't wait and explain things to you, but we're in a bit of a hurry to get back to Denver.''

Jack's gaze shifted to Lisa. She was so pale, her eyes dark with fear. It was all Jack could do to keep from yanking Hampton up by his collar and beating him bloody. But the way the man held on to Lisa with one hand and kept the other in his pocket had Jack worried. He could have a gun or knife in that pocket—Lord knows, Jack had his own .38 tucked into the back of his belt. But Lisa was much too close to chance any sudden moves.

"I got your note," he said, trying to tell her with his eyes that he understood she hadn't left on her own. "And your message. Not that I mind leftover shrimp, but this was kinda sudden, wasn't it?"

"Jack—"

"Yes, well," Roger said. "Do you think you could help us out of this mud? We really do need to be on our way."

Jack scratched his chin and studied the back end of the car. "You got yourself stuck in there pretty good, didn't you? Not to worry. We'll have more help here any minute. Meanwhile, Lisa's getting cold." He took a step toward her and held out his hand. "Come get in my rig where it's warm."

"She's fine," Roger said quickly. "Aren't you, darling?"

"She's shivering. Where's your coat, Lisa?"

"I…I'm afraid we left in such a hurry that I didn't bring it."

"I noticed your purse was still there, too. Come on. I'll take you back to the house to get them."

"She's not going anywhere."

Jack's jaw hardened. "Not with you, she's not. Let her go, Hampton."

"Jack, no, he's—"

"Shut up." Roger jerked on her arm.

Lisa stumbled into Roger, then righted herself. "It's no use, Roger. It isn't going to work."

Roger very much feared she was right. This lazy-talking cowboy wasn't going to help them out of the ditch. Roger could tell by the look in the man's eyes that he wasn't buying any of their story.

But Roger was too desperate to simply give up.

"She's right," Jack said. "It's not going to work. You're not taking her anywhere, Hampton. You might as well let her go."

"She wants to go with me. Don't you, Lisa? Tell him." He squeezed her arm so hard she winced. "Tell him how badly you want to go home with me."

"I won't—"

"Remember our agreement, dear."

"I've heard enough," Jack said. He stepped forward and broke Roger's hold on Lisa's arm.

Livid and panicked, Roger pulled the gun from his pocket, but Jack was so close, almost on top of him, that Roger couldn't bring the gun up to fire. He swung with his right fist and took Jack by surprise.

Jack staggered back, swearing at himself for underestimating his opponent. Then he saw the gun and his blood chilled.

Lisa saw it, too. Saw Roger raise it and aim at Jack's chest. She screamed. "No!" She swung both her arms upward and knocked his aim skyward just as the gun went off.

With a snarl, Roger backhanded her. The blow

stunned her and knocked her off balance. She fell into the dirty mound of snow at the side of the road.

Before Roger could take aim at Jack again, Jack roared in rage and dived, catching him around the waist and taking them both to the ground. To hell with the gun in his belt, Jack thought through a red haze. He wanted to pummel the bastard with his bare hands.

Roger rolled and came up on his knees. Once again he swung hard with his right fist.

Jack dodged, taking only a glancing blow to the shoulder. While the man's guard was down, Jack threw a solid punch to his gut and followed with a quick series to the head and face. Just as he took him by the collar and reared back to hit him again, someone caught his fist in midair.

"He's done for," Trey said.

Jack blinked to clear the fury and sweat from his eyes and saw that Trey was right. Hampton's eyes rolled back and he went limp. Jack let go of his collar and let the bastard fall facedown in the mud.

"Here." He pulled the gun from the back of his belt and handed it to Trey. "Keep an eye on him."

Stoney was helping Lisa to her feet.

Jack was at her side in an instant. "Lisa, honey, are you all right? Are you hurt?"

"Jack." With a glad cry, she threw herself into his arms and peppered his face with kisses. "Oh, Jack, I prayed you'd come. I was so scared. He had a gun and he threatened to hurt the baby and I didn't know what else to do but hope Stoney realized I was trying to tell him something was wrong. I couldn't put anything in the note because Roger dictated it. Oh, God, he said he'd kill you."

"It's all right now. I'm fine." At least he would be just as soon as his heart left his throat. And as soon as his hands quit shaking. And just as soon as he got a good solid taste of her, which he did right then. He tasted cold and fear, but also, incredibly, along with the sweet honeyed taste that was Lisa, he tasted...joy. "And you're fine." He stopped and kissed her again, just to reassure himself. "You are fine, aren't you?"

She nodded. "I'm cold and wet from the snow, but—"

"Here." Jack stripped off his sheepskin jacket and placed it around her shoulders. "Let's get you to the house so you can get out of those wet clothes."

He carried her to his rig and started the engine to warm up the interior. By then County Sheriff Dane Powell had pulled up. While Jack rolled down his window and spoke with him, Lisa huddled gratefully beneath Jack's coat and relished the warm air blasting from the heater.

The sheriff had been only a few miles away when Stoney's call had come in, she learned. Jack told the sheriff what had happened.

"Ms. Hampton." Sheriff Powell tugged on the brim of his hat. "I'll need to take your statement. The sooner we do it, the fresher everything will be in your mind."

Before Lisa could answer, Jack spoke. "I'm going to take her to the hospital to get checked over."

"Oh, Jack," Lisa protested. "That's not necessary."

"He hit you," Jack said, practically growling.

"Yes, he hit me, and I'll have a bruise on my cheek. That's not worth a trip to the hospital."

"You fell."

"I landed in deep snow on my hands and knees. If you want the truth," she said, smiling, "that's the first time I've been able to lie on my stomach in months. If it hadn't been so cold and wet, it would have felt good. My back actually quit aching for a minute. I don't need a doctor, Jack."

"But—"

"This baby is important to me. If I thought for a minute either one of us was injured, I'd be begging for a doctor."

Jack heaved a sigh. "All right. If you're sure."

"I'm sure. All I really want right now is a hot shower."

Jack and the sheriff spoke for a few more minutes.

The sheriff said, "Let me get this fellow into a ccll, then I'll either send one of my deputies out to get Ms. Hampton's statement or I'll come myself."

"Thanks, Dane." Jack shook his hand.

The sheriff placed Roger under arrest, handcuffed him and read him his rights.

"I never thought I was a vindictive person," Lisa said as she watched the sheriff stuff Roger into the back seat of his patrol car, "but that's one of the sweetest sights I've ever seen."

Jack merely grunted in response. He would have preferred a hearse. "Let's go home and get you into a hot shower."

"And those are the sweetest *words* I've ever *heard.*"

"Then come here. You're too far away." He helped her slide across the seat until he had her pressed up against his side with his arm around her. "That's better. Now we can go home."

Home, Lisa thought with relief and longing. But it wasn't her home. A huge wave of sadness swamped her. Her troubles with Roger seemed to be over now. The thought of returning to Denver, to her house there, left her feeling empty inside. How was she supposed to leave Jack? Yet what excuse could she use to stay?

He pulled up at the back door and carried her into the house.

"This is really getting to be a habit, you carrying me. Don't get me wrong," she told him, wrapping her arms around his neck. "I like it. But I can walk, Jack."

"Humor me, okay? When I realized he'd made you leave with him..." Jack stopped just inside the back door and rested his forehead against hers. "I don't ever want to be that scared again."

Lisa pressed her lips to his. "Neither do I."

"Feel better?" Jack had hovered outside the bathroom door while Lisa showered. Not because he thought she might need him, but because he needed to be close to her.

Wrapped in her long terry-cloth robe and toweling her hair dry, Lisa halted in her bedroom doorway. At the sight of Jack sitting on the edge of her bed, obviously waiting for her, her heart skipped a beat. "Much," she said in answer to his question.

Jack rose and stood before her, devouring her with his eyes. "I've got lunch, if you're interested."

Her stomach chose that moment to growl. She smiled. "I guess I'm interested."

He cupped her face in both hands and kissed her,

his tongue sliding in to dance along hers. "Are you sure you're all right?"

Lisa leaned against him and rested her head on his shoulder. "I am now."

Tell her, Jack thought. *Tell her you're in love with her.* But when he opened his mouth to say the words, what came out was, "I'll be downstairs." *Coward.*

As he went downstairs and left her alone to get dressed, he knew that, yes, it was pure cowardice that kept him from telling her he loved her. What if she hadn't meant what she'd said last night when she thought he was asleep? Maybe it was just one of those things women said when the sex was good. Maybe she was just grateful for the help he'd given her. Wasn't she always thanking him for something? Maybe that was all it was. Gratitude.

So ask her if she meant it.

Oh, yeah, sure. Hell, if he had the nerve to do that, he'd just up and tell her how he felt.

Okay. He would take the rest of the day to work out the words. After Dane came, took her statement and left, Jack would carry her up to bed— No. He would take her home with him. He wanted her in his bed, where she belonged. He would tell her there. That would be better.

When she came downstairs a half hour later, she looked refreshed, but she was still a little pale. Jack didn't like it. He'd made soup and sandwiches, and watched her eat.

"I could have lost you today," he said.

At his words Lisa's breath eased out and she couldn't get it back for a long moment. "I didn't know you wanted to keep me."

"I'm sorry. Maybe that didn't sound right. But I'm not ready to see the last of you."

Her heart thudded. "You're not?"

"After last night, you have to ask?"

She swallowed. Her face grew hot. "Last night was..."

"Yeah." He reached across the table and clasped her hand. "It was."

Suddenly the dull ache in her back sharpened.

"What's wrong?" Jack asked instantly.

She rubbed at the pain. "My back. Whew. It hurts."

Jack stood so fast his chair nearly toppled over. "That's it. We're getting you to the doctor. Now."

The ache was growing stronger. "I don't think I'm going to argue with you."

Within minutes they'd put on their coats, grabbed Lisa's purse and medical file and were on their way.

They didn't make it.

Chapter Twelve

It was thirteen miles of rough gravel road from the house to the paved county highway that led to town. Telling himself he was being expedient rather than reckless, Jack made it in twenty minutes.

"How are you doing?" He pulled out onto the highway and headed north for Hope Springs.

When Lisa didn't answer, he looked over at her and felt the blood drain from his head. "Lisa?"

With her head pushed back hard against the headrest and her hands gripping her belly, she gasped. "I think...Jack, I think the baby's coming."

His mouth went dry. "You're in labor?"

After a long moment she eased. "It came on so fast."

"Okay." He swallowed, licked his lips. "Okay, just hang on. We'll be at the hospital in less than thirty minutes."

Barely a minute later another fierce pain gripped her. "I don't think," she managed between gritted teeth, "the baby's going to wait that long."

Jack checked the speedometer. He was doing seventy-five. "I know it seems like it—"

"You do, huh?"

Making allowances for the fact that she was in pain, he ignored the tone of sarcasm in her voice.

"It takes time. We've got time." He hoped they had time. The road was straight, clear and dry. He pressed down on the accelerator.

"No." She let out a high keening moan. "Now. The baby's coming *now*."

Oh, God. "Okay. Okay." He slowed down and pulled off onto the shoulder. He could at least get her more comfortable. "I've got blankets. Sit tight. I'll make a bed for you in the back. Just...just pant. Like they do on TV."

He grabbed his cell phone and hopped out of the rig. By the time he reached the rear door he had dialed 911. He climbed in the back and, one-handed while he held the phone to his ear, dragged his toolbox out of the way and arranged the two blankets he kept for emergencies. If ever there was an emergency, this was it.

He gave the 911 operator his name and location. "We're having a baby out here. We need an ambulance."

"How far apart are the contractions, sir?"

"Lisa, they want to know how far apart the contractions are."

"Apart?" she said with a grunt of pain. "They're supposed to be apart? Oh, God, I've got to push."

"Don't push. Not yet. Not yet." Into the phone he said, "I gotta go," and tossed the phone aside.

Within seconds he was at Lisa's side, lifting her from the seat and carrying her around to the back cargo area of the rig. He made sure all the doors and windows were closed so there wouldn't be a draft. He tore off his coat and stuffed it behind her head and shoulders, with her hips resting on the folded blankets.

Nothing was sterile. How could she have a baby in the back of his rig?

It couldn't be helped, so they would just do the best they could. God, she was hurting, and it was killing him.

Newspaper. Wasn't that supposed to be pretty sterile? Trey had brought the newspaper with him that morning to read while Jack drove them to the section of fence that needed repair. He grabbed the paper from the back seat and placed it next to Lisa.

"How you doing?" He knew as he asked that it was a stupid question.

"I don't know," she huffed out. "I think...I think I'm scared. It's too soon. The baby's not due yet."

No, the baby wasn't due yet. And maybe it wasn't coming right this minute the way she thought it was. This was her first baby. Maybe the sudden labor pains were just panicking her. But even if she was right and the baby was coming right now, Jack felt suddenly calm. Deep down inside he knew that this baby and this woman were going to be fine.

He took her hand. "Don't worry, cupcake, everything is going to be all right."

"You're not going to be able to call me that much longer."

From the corner of his eye Jack saw Dane Powell slow down in the oncoming lane. He pulled off and parked directly across the highway from them and got out. "Need help?" he called through the back window of Jack's rig.

"Get in and drive," Jack called back. "We're having a baby."

Lisa's eyes filled. She wondered if Jack realized he'd said *we*. She wondered if he knew that he was grinning like a new daddy. Then she couldn't wonder about anything but how to get through the newest pain that threatened to tear her apart.

Jack turned back to her. "Ah, baby, I'm sorry it hurts. I'm going to get your pants off you now, okay?"

Lisa groaned, knowing that even as she did, the sheriff—a virtual stranger to her—was climbing into the driver's seat. "Why does childbirth...have to be so...undignified?"

"Humph," Jack said. "Don't worry about Dane. I imagine he's seen a naked woman before. Besides, he's not even looking." Jack removed her shoes and set them aside, then waited until the contraction eased before gently working her maternity slacks off. So as not to make a big deal out of it, he took her panties at the same time.

"You two ready for me to drive?" Dane called from the driver's seat.

"Go," Jack ordered. "Where the hell's the ambulance?"

Dane put the rig into gear and pulled out. "About five minutes before you called 911, Homer Blevins plowed head-on into Mabel Ditwiler in front of the high school."

"Homer Blevins?" Jack's attention was on Lisa, but he hoped his conversation with Dane might distract her even a little from her pain. "What's he doing with a driver's license? He's blind as a bat."

"He doesn't have a license. He found the place where his daughter hides the car keys and decided to go for a spin. He got banged up some, and Mrs. Ditwiler says she's going to sue the city, but all in all it could have been a lot worse. Anyway, the ambulance is delayed, so you get me. Now," he added, giving it the gas, "let's get this new mama to the hospital."

"Sheriff?" Lisa said, panting.

"Yo."

"Thank you."

"You're more than welcome." He smiled into the rearview mirror. "I'm here to serve."

"Okay, now," Jack said to Lisa. "I need to see what's going on." Gently he eased her knees up and apart and braced her feet against his knees. His heart knocked hard beneath his ribs. "Yep, we've got a baby on the way. I see the top of the head. Are you panting?"

She started panting again. The next contraction came in a matter of seconds as the vehicle gathered speed and raced down the highway.

"Go ahead, cupcake," Jack encouraged. "Holler all you want. This is no time to be stoic."

It didn't make him feel any better when she gave in to a deep groan. He would gladly have taken the pain away from her and into his own body if he could.

Her face was flushed and sheened in sweat, her hair matted against her skull. He'd never seen a more beautiful woman in his life.

She groaned again. "I need to push."

"Don't push yet. Don't push."

"How's it going back there?" Dane called.

Jack took another look. "I can see the top of the head."

"Don't let her push until the head is out."

"You've done this before?"

"I've seen a film."

"Ah, an expert, then. Here's the head." Supporting it in both hands, Jack grinned up at Lisa. "Almost there, cupcake."

She snarled at him. "You *are* going to stop calling me that."

"With the next contraction, push."

He barely got the words out before the next contraction gripped her. Her face contorted into a mask of pain and effort. The long rolling groan came as if from the depths of her soul, as if her life depended on getting it out.

"We have a shoulder," Jack told her. "One more time, honey, push hard. You can do it."

Panting, gasping, Lisa pushed with all her might. The second shoulder appeared, and the rest of the baby slipped out into Jack's hands.

"My God." His vision blurred. Grinning so hard his jaws ached, he held the baby up for Lisa to see. "You were right. She's a girl, and she's breathing and beautiful."

Lisa sobbed once, then laughed.

"Here you go, little cupcake," he crooned to the baby. He pushed Lisa's top up out of the way and placed the baby on her bare stomach.

"Jacqueline," Lisa murmured, stroking the top of the baby's head.

"What?"

Lisa met Jack's gaze steadily. "I'm naming her Jacqueline."

Jack had to blink to clear his vision. "Lisa...I...don't know what to say."

"Everything okay back there?" Dane called.

Lisa swallowed. "Jacqueline Dana."

With a smile that wobbled, Jack repeated the name. "Jacqueline Dana. You hear that, Dane? This little cupcake's name is Jacqueline Dana."

In the driver's seat, Sheriff Dane Powell had to swallow three times before he could speak around the lump of emotion in his throat. Then all he could manage to say was, "Wow."

"I want to hold her," Lisa begged Jack.

"I'm sorry, honey, the cord's not long enough. This is as far as she goes for now." He leaned over them both and pressed his lips to Lisa's. "Congratulations, Mommy."

Again came that burst of emotion that was both a sob and laughter.

"You were fantastic." He kissed her again. "You were wonderful." And again.

When they reached the hospital fifteen minutes later, they were met by Dr. Will Carver, two orderlies and two nurses. Probably ninety percent of the staff currently on duty at the hospital.

Jack had already wrapped the baby in a clean blanket and placed her back on Lisa's stomach. Now he eased the two of them into his arms and scooted out of the vehicle to place them gently on the gurney.

The doctor and nurses were sure taking their own sweet time, Jack thought, considering *he* had done the hard part. Dane had long since left to hitch a ride out to his vehicle. It had been nearly two hours since they'd taken Lisa and the baby away from him. Making him feel unnecessary. As if they no longer needed him. As if mother and child might be better off without him.

The nurses said he wasn't sterile. They didn't know the half of it. He'd been out sweating over a fence all morning, then tussling with Hampton on that muddy road. Not to mention delivering a baby in the back of his rig. Sterile? Hell, he wasn't even clean.

He worried that he might have harmed Lisa or the baby somehow because of it, but the nurse who had barred him from Lisa's room told him it looked as though everything was fine. She found a spare set of scrubs and made him wash up, so here he was, pacing the hallway, feeling naked as a jaybird in borrowed pea-green clothes—not even fresh peas at that, but sickly-looking canned peas—that looked like pajamas and were three inches too short for his legs. And the things were damned drafty, he thought with irritation.

Finally Dr. Carver came out of Lisa's room into the corridor where Jack was pacing. "Congratulations, Jack. You did a good job. You get tired of raising cattle, you might think about taking up midwifery."

"Real funny, Will. Are they all right? Lisa and the baby?"

"You mean Lisa and little Jacqueline Dana?" Will grinned. "They're both fine. The baby was about two weeks early, but so far there are no complications from that. Her lungs are fully formed—that was my biggest concern. I want to keep them both for two or three days. When they go home, Lisa will need plenty of help."

"She'll have it," Jack vowed. Belinda and Ace would be home tomorrow, and with them, the kids and Donna. Belinda and Donna would be there day and night to give Lisa all the help she needed.

And she won't need you anymore.

He wouldn't think about that. Couldn't bear to think about it, because he knew it was true. She wouldn't need him. Didn't need him now. "Can I see her?"

"Sure." The doctor slapped Jack on the back. "Now that you're cleaned up."

Jack stood before the door to her room and felt sweat dampen his palms. Hell, he'd been steady as a rock when the baby was born. Now that the scary part was over, he was nervous.

He wiped his palms down the thighs of the borrowed scrubs, took a deep breath and entered her room.

And stopped dead in his tracks, spellbound. She was nursing the baby. The sight of it, so beautiful, so maternal, took his breath away. The look of love in her eyes as she gazed down at her daughter swelled his throat closed.

They had cleaned the baby up. She was still red and wrinkled, but it was the red of healthy newborn skin. Her hair, thick and dark, gleamed. She was wearing a diaper now. One tiny red fist kneaded her mother's milk-pale breast.

Suddenly, as if she sensed his presence—he knew he hadn't made a sound, hadn't been capable of it—Lisa looked up and smiled. "Jack."

"Hi. How do you feel?"

Her smile widened. "Like I just gave birth."

Jack rushed to her side. "Are you in pain? Can't they give you—"

"I'm fine, Jack. They already gave me something for the pain—now that the worst part's over. Oh, Jack, you were wonderful out there. I don't know what we'd have done without you."

He swallowed and looked down at the baby. "I can't believe you named her after me. I'm...humbled."

They were silent for a moment, both watching the baby as her mouth went slack. When Lisa's nipple popped free of the baby's mouth, Lisa and Jack both turned suddenly shy. Lisa pulled the hospital gown up to cover herself, while Jack strode to the window and looked out through the blinds.

"Dane—" Jack stopped and cleared his throat. "Dane says not to worry about giving him your statement. He'll talk to you later, whenever you feel up to it."

"Tell him thank-you. Just as long as waiting doesn't mean Roger goes free."

Jack's eyes narrowed. "Not a chance. There's a question as to whether or not the judge will even set bail. Flight risk, no ties to the area—other than you, and you're his victim."

"I'm sure Roger has already called his grandfather. Something will be worked out. He won't sit in jail long. I can guarantee it."

Jack turned back and stood beside her bed. "He won't get near you again. *I* can guarantee *that*." He looked down at the baby again. "God, she's beautiful."

"She is, isn't she?"

"She's got your mouth. Your nose."

A nurse poked her head in the door. "Are you ready for me to take her to the nursery?"

Jack could see the conflict in Lisa's face. She was exhausted, but she didn't want to let go of the baby. Finally she sighed and let the nurse take her.

"I'll go," Jack said. "So you can sleep."

She looked up at him, the lines of fatigue around her eyes and mouth proclaiming her exhaustion. "Will you come back tomorrow?"

That she thought she had to ask told Jack he'd been right; things were different between them now. He felt suddenly awkward. Unnecessary. But he knew he wouldn't be able to stay away from her. "Sure. What do you want me to bring you from the house?"

"Oh." She laughed. "Everything. Clothes, nightgown, robe, slippers, toothbrush, deodorant, under—"

"Everything." So she still needed him, at least for this. "You got it, Mama."

Lisa watched him leave. She had never expected to find a man like him, a man she could love with her whole heart, a man with whom she could share her daughter. But as sleep claimed her, she worried about the new distance she sensed between them.

The thought of going home to his empty house held no appeal for Jack. He was still high on the birth of Lisa's baby, even as the thought that she might no longer need him weighed on his mind. He had a need to be around family.

He would go see Rachel and Grady and the kids. He hadn't seen his sister and her family, or Ace's boys, since before the blizzard. Before Lisa.

Besides, he wasn't about to drive all the way home in pea-green pajamas.

He headed north out of town and drove to Standing Elk Ranch, where he promptly agreed to explain his odd manner of dress in exchange for supper.

After he left—in his freshly laundered clothes—and after the boys were in bed, Rachel turned to Grady. "I still can't get over Jack delivering Lisa's baby. Did you pick up on what I picked up on?"

Grady grinned. "He's nuts about her."

"Head over heals in love with her."

"I'd say so."

Rachel laughed. With her arms spread wide, she fell back on the bed. "My big bad brother has finally fallen in love. I can't wait to meet her."

Back at the Flying Ace, Jack went to the main house and up to Lisa's room. He'd promised he would take her things to her. She might not need him for much anymore, but she at least needed him for this. And there were also her other belongings in the trunk of her car at the garage in town. She might need those when she got out of the hospital. He could take care of that for her.

Afterward…well, afterward, he would take a step back, get his bearings and see what was what. If she didn't need him anymore, didn't want him…

Chapter Thirteen

Lisa spent the early hours the next morning holding her daughter, staring at her, marveling at her. Getting her to nurse and praying her milk would come in soon. One of the nurses helped her give Jacqueline a bath, and there were lessons in diaper changing.

Wouldn't her friends at the ad agency get a kick out of her excitement over changing a diaper.

Every few minutes as the morning progressed, Lisa glanced toward the door. She did it unconsciously at first, before realizing what she was doing. But it took no great thought to know she was looking for Jack.

Would he come?

Of course he would. He'd said he would bring her clothes and things. If nothing else, he would keep his word.

But she wanted him to come because he wanted to see her, not just to run an errand.

He'd been so wonderful yesterday, so kind and gentle. So loving. She had felt so close to him—until he'd entered her hospital room and she'd sensed a distance between them that hadn't been there before, not even the day they'd met.

"Is he tired of us, do you think?" she asked her daughter.

It could be. She had a team of nurses to look after her now, and tomorrow Belinda would be home. Maybe Jack was ready to wash his hands of her. She'd been such a burden to him she really couldn't blame him. But she prayed she was wrong.

Finally, around ten o'clock, he arrived. With him he brought her suitcase and a beautiful arrangement of pink carnations surrounded by baby's breath.

"Oh, Jack, how pretty! You shouldn't have."

Jack felt the hole in the pit of his stomach, the hole he'd felt yesterday when he'd realized she no longer needed him, grow larger. *You shouldn't have.* Wasn't that what you said to a casual acquaintance? It sounded that way to him.

"You've done so much for me already," she said.

The hole in his gut got bigger. "Well," he said with a shrug, trying to put a good face on it, "you have to share them with the little cupcake there. How is she?"

Lisa looked down at the yawning baby in her arms. "She's tired. We've had a busy morning, what with feedings and baths and diaper changes and all."

"Maybe I should go and let the two of you get some rest."

"Oh, but you just got here," Lisa protested.

"I'll, uh, come back later."

He left so fast Lisa was dazed. The tears came

without warning. He didn't want her anymore. Didn't want anything to do with her. But he was such a nice and decent man he probably would come back, simply because he'd promised.

"Oh, Jack." He was slipping away from her and she didn't know why, or how to stop it.

Later that morning the florist brought more flowers—from Dane, from Belinda and her husband, who weren't even home from Hawaii yet, and even a bouquet from Roger's parents, with a separate arrangement from his grandfather, which included a note swearing Lisa would never have to worry about Roger bothering her again.

In the afternoon Trey and Stoney came. Lisa thought it was sweet of them, and they made quite a fuss over the baby. Trey brought her a pink teddy bear, and Stoney a stuffed bunny rabbit.

"Oh, thank you!" Lisa exclaimed. "Her first toys."

Trey grinned, while Stoney blushed.

Just before supper a beautiful, black-haired, blue-eyed woman came to her room, and Lisa knew instantly that this must be Jack's sister. She was a petite feminine version of Jack and Trey.

"Hi. I hope you don't mind my dropping in. I'm Rachel Lewis, Jack's sister. I wanted to introduce myself and bring you some..." She glanced around the room and grinned. "Oh, my. Some flowers."

"How sweet of you," Lisa said, thrilled to meet her. "I'm so glad you came."

"I couldn't stay away. Jack came for supper last night and told us what happened. He said you were all right, but I had to make sure for myself. Belinda would have my hide. She might have it, anyway, because I haven't even so much as called you since you got here.''

''I imagine you've been a little busy. Haven't your nephews been staying with you?''

Rachel laughed and rolled her eyes.

Rachel stayed and visited for nearly half an hour. She left when the nurse brought Lisa's supper tray. By then, Lisa felt as if she'd known the woman her entire life.

Lisa had no sooner finished eating when Belinda arrived.

''You're here!'' Lisa declared, more glad than she could say to see her best friend at last.

''You didn't wait for me,'' Belinda scolded. ''You weren't supposed to have the baby until I got home. But what the heck, I love you, anyway.'' She enveloped Lisa in a big hug. ''Are you all right?'' she demanded. ''We heard the most incredible story about Jack delivering the baby.''

''It's true. He was wonderful.''

''Well, where is he? And where is this alleged baby?''

Lisa felt her hope shrivel and did her best to hide it. If Belinda was asking where Jack was, then he hadn't come with her. This morning he had stayed barely five minutes, and she hadn't seen him since. She knew he had work to do, and it was a long drive between the ranch and town. But she had hoped...

''Could I get an introduction here?''

Lisa looked at the man at the foot of her bed. The family resemblance was stunning. He and Jack could have been twins. The two of them and Trey could have been triplets, so alike were they.

"You're Ace." She couldn't help but smile as she held out a hand to him. His grip was firm and warm, his hand as callused as Jack's. "I can't tell you how glad I am to meet the man who could get this one—" she put her other hand on Belinda's shoulder "—to the altar."

"And you must be Lisa," Ace responded with an easy smile. "I'm glad to finally meet you, too. It sounds like you've had an, uh, eventful stay so far."

Lisa chuckled. "I'll say. You folks in Wyoming sure know how to show a lady a good time."

"Oh, yeah, right." Belinda took off her coat and tossed it on the nearby chair. "Car accidents, amnesia, blizzards, power outages, kidnapping and roadside childbirth. Be glad we don't really like you, or we'd have thrown in something really cool, like an influenza outbreak, to cap things off."

"And all this without your even having to be here," Lisa added. "I can't wait for you to see Jackie."

"Who?"

"My daughter. Jacqueline Dana."

"Oh, my God." Belinda looked dumbstruck. "You named her after... I think I'd better sit down."

"You knew everything else that's happened. Didn't Jack tell you?"

"He didn't say a word." Belinda looked at Ace, who shook his head. "That rat. I'll murder him for not telling me something that important."

"Give the guy a break," Ace said. "We haven't even seen him yet, only talked to him on the phone. We just got in and haven't even picked up the boys yet. Belinda couldn't wait to see you."

A moment later the nurse brought Jacqueline to the room.

Ace could see he wasn't needed or wanted here. No one even seemed to remember he was there. "I'll leave the two—three—of you to visit. Lisa, it was nice meeting you."

"Ace, thank you for coming," she said earnestly. "And thank you, both of you, for letting me stay at your ranch. I can't tell you how much it's meant to me."

"You're welcome," he told her. "But don't start thinking of leaving. I know for a fact that Belinda won't let you."

"He's right of course," Belinda said when her husband left. "You're staying with us until you decide what you want to do, and I won't hear any arguments. And if you don't let me hold that baby in the next two minutes, I'm going to hit you over the head and make off with her. I'll change her name to Lelani and tell everyone we brought her home from Hawaii."

Laughing, Lisa carefully placed her daughter into the arms of the best friend she'd ever had.

"Now," Belinda said, "suppose you tell me why you named this beautiful angel after a man you barely know. And don't tell me it's because he delivered her. There's got to be more to it than that. Spill it, girl."

"Oh, Belinda..." Lisa broke down and cried.

The Flying Ace headquarters was a madhouse of confusion that night when Ace, Belinda, their sons and housekeeper returned.

Jason, Grant and Clay were wild about having their parents home and being back in their own house. They regaled their parents with all their exploits—the snow fort they'd built in the backyard at Standing Elk, the snowball war they'd had with Grady and Rachel, the day they got out of school because of the blizzard.

"Man, it was cool!" Jason exclaimed.

Jack watched it all with an ache in his chest. For the first time in his life, he truly envied his older brother.

It took two hours for the boys to wind down enough to go to bed. When they finally did, Ace and Jack settled in the office so Jack could fill Ace in on ranch business.

"That's pretty damned interesting," Ace said an hour later.

"What is?"

"You've just talked for a solid hour about the blizzard, the cattle, the fences, and you haven't said a single word about Lisa. I gotta wonder about that."

Jack shrugged. "I told Belinda all of that over the phone last night, and you've met her. Nothing else to say."

Ace leaned back and placed his hands behind his head. "Except, according to Rachel, you love her."

Jack shot him a narrow-eyed glare. "She's right. I've loved Rachel since she was a kid."

"Very funny, bro. I'm talking about Lisa."

"There's nothing to talk about." Jack wasn't ready to bare his soul to Ace or anyone.

"Isn't there?"

"No." Jack stood and headed for the door. "No, there isn't."

Jack would have kept on walking, but Belinda was suddenly blocking the doorway.

"Oh," she said with a gleam in her eye, "I think there is. I think there's a lot more to talk about." She placed one hand squarely in the middle of Jack's chest and shoved. "Sit down."

"Well, hell," Jack muttered. But he sat, because there was no getting around Belinda when she got that steely-eyed look about her.

"Very good," she said, as if he were a puppy who'd just piddled on the paper instead of the floor. "The first thing you should be aware of before you start denying things is that Lisa and I are *very* good friends. She tells me *everything.*"

"And your point is…?"

"My point is, what is this nonsense about you not being able to love a woman and not knowing how to be a husband or father?"

"She said that?" Ace asked his wife.

"I had to browbeat her to get it out of her."

"You browbeat her?" Jack cried, outraged. "That woman has been through pure hell this past week. You had no business—"

"Looks like Rachel was right." Ace's grin was huge. "He's nuts about her."

"I've heard enough." Jack moved as if to get up, until he saw the look in Belinda's eyes.

"I'll just come after you."

"Look, you two," Jack said with what little patience he had left. "No offense, but this is none of your business."

"No offense taken," Belinda said sweetly.

When Belinda got sweet, a man had better look out.

"However," Ace said, "I'm remembering a certain early-morning trip to the family cemetery a while back."

"Early-morning kidnapping was more like it," Belinda corrected.

Jack groaned. The two of them, Ace and Belinda, had been eaten alive with guilt for having feelings for each other, each of them letting the ghost of Belinda's sister, Ace's late wife, stand between them. Jack had finally gotten fed up watching them tap-dance around their feelings for each other. Never were two people more suited to each other or more in love than they had been, but they were letting Cathy stand between them as if she were still alive. In pure frustration Jack had dragged them to the cemetery one morning and pointed to Cathy's grave, demanding that they acknowledge that she was dead and they weren't.

It hadn't been the nicest thing he'd ever done, but the results were there before him now—a man and woman, husband and wife, deeply in love and more suited to each other than any two people in the world. Jack had no regrets.

Except now it looked as though they were going to use that little incident as an excuse to butt into his life.

"So," Belinda said, "we feel we owe it to you to get to the bottom of your problems."

"I don't have any problems." The lie had come way too easily.

"You *are* the problem," Ace said tersely, "if you believe any of that garbage about not being able to be a good husband and father."

"Hell, Ace, what do I know about that sort of thing? You know I never had a father at all until I was twelve, and then the one I got…well, King Wilder never won any prizes for fatherhood."

"So what?" Ace cried. "I had the same lousy father you did. Are you saying I'm no good at raising my sons?"

"No!" Jack stared in shock. "Of course not. You're a great father."

"Hallelujah," Belinda said. "If Ace is a great father—and he's the best—and you and he had the same father, then you've got no excuse in that department, buster. Maybe Rachel was wrong. Maybe you really don't love Lisa. Or maybe you just don't want to raise another man's child as your own."

It was on the tip of Jack's tongue to protest that Jacqueline Dana was not another man's child, she was *his*. Hadn't he felt her move in her mother's womb? Hadn't he helped bring her into the world? Weren't his hands the first touch she'd ever known?

But he bit back the words and pushed himself from his chair. "I have to think."

"Think real hard," Belinda called after him as he left the room. "Before you lose the best thing that ever happened to you."

Ace and Belinda listened as Jack's footsteps faded, then the back door slammed.

"Do you think we were too hard on him?" Belinda asked.

"Not nearly as hard as he's obviously been on himself. At least he's thinking now. With any luck, he's thinking straight."

"It's about damn time," Belinda muttered.

The next morning after he finished his chores, Jack stood beside his rig and stared at the pile of Lisa's belongings in the back. He'd gone by the garage yesterday after leaving the hospital and gotten them from the trunk of her car. Two more suitcases, several boxes, a portable crib, a computer. The trunk had been crammed.

He supposed he should haul it all up to the house and unload it, so she would have it there when they brought her home later that day. She was supposed to be discharged around two.

He'd overheard some of the arrangements last night that Belinda and Donna were making. Donna was going to move upstairs into the guest room so they could put Lisa and the baby in Donna's room downstairs off the kitchen. It seemed they'd decided Lisa didn't need to be climbing stairs all day.

After witnessing firsthand what she'd gone through giving birth, Jack had no quarrel with that. If he had his way, she wouldn't get out of bed for the next month.

But dammit, he didn't want her in the downstairs room off the kitchen in his brother's house. He wanted her in *his* house. He wanted...hell, he wanted too damn much.

What he wanted most just then was to know where he stood with her. And by God, he was tired of guessing. He was going to find out.

When Jack got to the hospital, he figured he had the worst case of cold feet in history. But this was too important for him to let that stop him. He entered Lisa's room, ready to fight for his life, because no less than that was at stake.

"Jack, you came."

He nodded once. Her smile looked sad around the edges and scared the hell out of him. "I came. Lisa, I—"

"Would you do something for me?"

"Of course."

"I know I've asked too much of you already, but—"

"You've never asked anything of me. Whatever I've done, I've done because I wanted to."

"All right," she said slowly. "But this time I'm asking."

"All right, what is it?"

"Would you…" She paused and shifted the baby in her arms. "Would you hold Jacqueline Dana?"

Jack's heart gave a hard thump somewhere near his throat. Sweat broke out on his palms. "Hold her?" He was dying to hold her.

"Please? If you don't mind, that is."

He swallowed hard. "I…of course I don't mind. But it's been a while since I've held a baby that small. Shouldn't you get one of the nurses to hold her for you?"

"No. I want…I want to be able to tell her, when she's older, that the man who delivered her, the man she's named for, held her in his arms."

Everything inside Jack went numb. If that wasn't a goodbye, he didn't know what was. She was through with him. Or would be, once this was done. He wanted to throw back his head and howl in protest. He wanted to gnash his teeth. He wanted to weep.

Instead, he held out his arms. "Give her here," he said, his voice rough with emotion.

The ache in Lisa's throat grew almost unbearable as she placed her sleeping daughter in Jack's arms.

She'd made her decision last night. She would not try to hold on to him. He had already stepped back from her. Now Belinda was home, and there was no longer any reason for her to lean on him, to need him.

He had his own life to live. She had conveniently ignored that fact from the beginning. The blizzard had altered everything, sealing them together inside that little house.

But that was long past, and now that he didn't have to worry about her all the time, he could get back to his own life.

Seeing him hold the child he had delivered from her womb was the most precious sight in the world to her. The way he gazed down at the baby with so much love in his eyes. The way his callused hands held her so gently, one finger stroking her hair.

Oh, God, she was going to humiliate herself and fall apart if she didn't get a grip.

"Hello, little cupcake," he said softly to the baby. "How are you doing today? Are you being nice to your mama?" He eased down until he was sitting on the edge of Lisa's bed. "I guess the two of you don't need me anymore, huh? You've got all these nurses here at the hospital, and pretty soon you'll have your aunt Belinda and Donna and everybody else to look after you. Maybe someday your mama will tell you about conking herself out and losing her memory. You probably won't believe it, but it's true, I swear."

Jack was silent for a long time, just staring down at the baby in his arms.

No. He couldn't do this. He couldn't surrender without a fight. He stood and leaned down. "Take her." His voice came out more harshly than he'd intended.

"Jack, I'm sor—"

"Wait." He held up his hand, palm forward. "Wait. This is all sounding like a big goodbye scene, and before we go that far, I have a question to ask you.''

With her heart breaking, Lisa shifted the baby in her arms. ''A question?''

''That's right.'' He stood beside the bed and stuffed his hands into the front pockets of his jeans. ''The other night, when you thought I was asleep, did you mean what you said?''

He didn't need to explain. Lisa remembered perfectly what she'd whispered in the dark when she'd thought he was asleep.

''You were awake?''

He nodded. ''I was awake.''

Heat stung her cheeks. ''Why didn't you say anything?''

''I...I don't know. Did you mean it?''

She picked at an imaginary piece of lint on the baby's blanket. ''That you were the most loving man I'd ever dreamed of knowing? Yes.'' She looked up at him. ''I meant it.''

Jack balled his fists to keep from reaching for her. ''What about the rest? Did you mean that, too?''

She swallowed and held his gaze. ''Yes. I meant it.''

''You said...you said you loved me.''

''Yes. I did. Am I...am I alone in this?''

Slowly Jack took his hands from his pockets and sat on the edge of her bed. ''No.'' As he reached for her, his hands shook. ''No, you're not alone, Lisa. I love you. If you'll have me, you'll never be alone again, I swear it.''

Her eyes, those beautiful green eyes, filled with tears. ''Jack?''

''I love you, Lisa Hampton. I don't know anything

about being a husband, but if you'll help me, I'll learn. If love counts for anything, I've got it licked. As for her," he said, looking down at the baby and stroking her cheek with a fingertip, "I've been her slave from the minute she was born. Before that, even."

"Oh, Jack."

"I want us to get married. I want us, the three of us, to be a family. I want you and Jacqueline Dana to share my home, my life and my name. If you need to stand on your own, that's fine. Just let me stand beside you. If you want a large family, let me give you mine. If you want more children...marry me, Lisa. Marry me."

"Oh, Jack, yes, yes." She lay her head on his shoulder, with the baby cuddled between them, and wept tears of joy.

When Belinda and Ace arrived to take Lisa and Jacqueline home, they found Jack sitting in a chair holding the baby while Lisa stood beside them, dressed and running a brush through her hair.

"You're all ready?" Belinda asked.

Lisa whirled toward the door. "Belinda!"

"Good grief," Belinda said. "Lisa, you're... you're practically glowing."

"There's been a change of plans," Jack said.

"Oh, really?" Belinda asked, a slow smile starting across her face.

"Yes, really." Jack rose and stood beside Lisa, the baby in one arm, the other arm going around Lisa, and faced his brother and sister-in-law. "Lisa won't be going home with you. She's coming home with me."

"Well, now." Ace folded his arms across his chest. "Since Lisa doesn't have a father here to speak up for her, I guess that leaves it up to me. Are the two of you planning to live in sin?"

Lisa burst out laughing.

Jack raised an eyebrow. "Not that it's any of your business—"

"You wanna watch that, Jack," Belinda warned with a gleam in her eye.

"We're getting married," Lisa told them.

Belinda shouted. "Hallelujah!"

With their daughter cradled in one arm, Jack looked down at the woman who was his life. "Let's go home."

"Yes," she whispered. "Let's."

* * * * *

What's a single man to do when he finds a baby on his doorstep, and he learns the little heartbreaker is his? Watch Trey Wilder fall for his tiny daughter and the woman he hires to care for her! Watch for the next book in
THE WILDERS OF WYATT COUNTY
family saga miniseries as it continues in 2001, available only in Silhouette Special Edition.

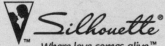

That's My Baby!

Don't miss these heartwarming stories coming to THAT'S MY BABY— only from Silhouette Special Edition.

August 2000:

WHEN BABY WAS BORN
by **Jodi O'Donnell** (SE #1339)

Sara was about to give birth—and couldn't remember anything except her name! But then a twist of fate brought dashing cowboy Cade McGivern to the rescue....

October 2000:

BACHELOR'S BABY PROMISE
by **Barbara McMahon** (SE #1351)

Jared Montgomery wasn't looking for love—until the handsome new father fell for the blue-eyed beauty who tenderly cared for his adorable baby girl.

THAT'S MY BABY!
Sometimes bringing up baby can bring surprises...and showers of love!

Available at your favorite retail outlet.

Silhouette ®

Where love comes alive ™

Through the darkness,
love illuminates the way home....

GINNA GRAY

THE
PRODIGAL
Daughter

Seven years ago
Maggie Malone lost
everything one hellish night
and left Ruby Falls, Texas, in
disgrace. Now Maggie has
come home.

Her father is dying
and so is their proud
family business. Maggie had once dreamed of
running the empire—and old dreams die hard. But
to claim them, she'll have to confront the father
who denies her, the family who resents her, the
secrets that surround her, the man who wants
her...and the treachery closing in on them all.

**Ginna Gray "is one of the most consistently
excellent writers in the genre today."
—*Romantic Times***

*On sale September 2000
wherever paperbacks are sold!*

**Don't miss
an exciting opportunity
to save on the purchase of
Harlequin and Silhouette books!**

Buy any two Harlequin or
Silhouette books and save
$10.00 off future Harlequin
and Silhouette purchases

OR

buy any three
Harlequin or Silhouette books
and save **$20.00 off** future
Harlequin and Silhouette purchases.

**Watch for details
coming in October 2000!**

PHQ400

Silhouette®

SPECIAL EDITION®

COMING NEXT MONTH

#1351 BACHELOR'S BABY PROMISE—Barbara McMahon
That's My Baby!
Jared Montgomery wasn't looking for love—until the tall, dark and handsome geologist fell for the blue-eyed beauty he hired to watch his baby girl. Could the winsome ways of nurturing schoolteacher Jenny Stratford transform this most stubborn of bachelors?

#1352 MARRYING A DELACOURT—Sherryl Woods
And Baby Makes Three: The Delacourts of Texas
Strong-willed Grace Foster had left the dashing but difficult Michael Delacourt when she'd realized he was married to his job. Now, to win her back, he was going to have to prove that love was his most important mission of all.

#1353 MILLIONAIRE TAKES A BRIDE—Pamela Toth
Here Come the Brides
When charming rogue Ryan Noble set his mind on taking a bride, he did just that. Trouble was, he claimed Sarah Daniels...the wrong twin! To make matters worse, his *un*intended bride's irresistible allure was stealing *his* heart.

#1354 A BUNDLE OF MIRACLES—Amy Frazier
Rugged police chief Ben Chase built an impenetrable exterior after his beloved Abbie Latham left town without explanation. Only a miracle could reunite these two soul mates separated by a painful secret. Was the bundled-up baby on Abbie's doorstep the sign they'd been waiting for?

#1355 HIDDEN IN A HEARTBEAT—Patricia McLinn
A Place Called Home
Primly proper Rebecca Dahlgren came to Wyoming to learn about her Native American heritage—not to fall for some irksome cattle rancher. But Luke Chandler's powerful presence and passionate kisses were arousing desires she couldn't ignore!

#1356 STRANGER IN A SMALL TOWN—Ann Roth
Single mom Alison O'Hara was struggling to make ends meet when brooding stranger Clint Strong became her new tenant. A few fiery embraces stirred up feelings she'd forgotten existed. But while Alison might have opened the door to her home, would she welome him into her heart?